DAVY JONES'
HAUNTED LOCKER

DAVY JONES' HAUNTED LOCKER

Great Ghost Stories of the Sea
Selected by Robert Arthur

Illustrated by Joseph Cellini

Random House · New York

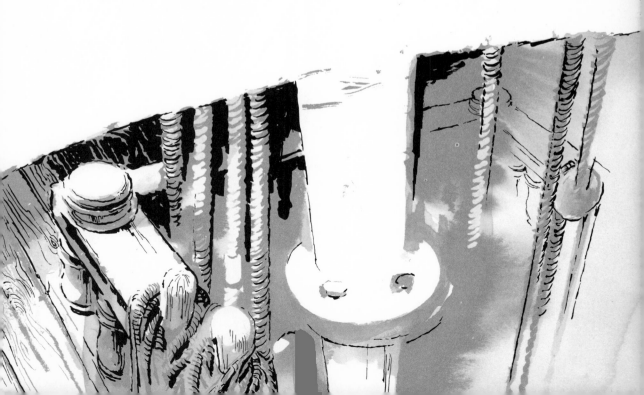

The editor wishes to thank the following for permission to reprint:

Arkham House—"Second Night Out" from *The Hounds of Tindalos* by Frank Belknap Long. Copyright, 1933, by The Popular Fiction Publishing Company; 1946, by Frank Belknap Long. "The Voice in the Night" from *Men of the Deep Waters* by William Hope Hodgson.

Robert Arthur—"Jabez O'Brien and Davy Jones' Locker" by Robert Arthur. © 1965 by Mercury Press, Inc. for *The Magazine of Fantasy and Science Fiction*.

Brandt & Brandt—"The Hemp" from *The Selected Works of Stephen Vincent Benét*. Copyright, 1916, by Stephen Vincent Benét; copyright renewed, 1934, by Stephen Vincent Benét.

J. M. Dent & Sons Ltd.—"The Roll Call of the Reef" from *Wandering Heath* by Sir Arthur Quiller-Couch (Charles Scribner's Sons, 1895).

Arthur J. A. Dudley, executor of the Estate of Miss Lissie Hodgson—"The Stone Ship" from *The Luck of the Strong* by William Hope Hodgson.

Dowager Lady Dunsany and David McKay Company, Inc.—"One August in the Red Sea" by Lord Dunsany from *Jorkens Remembers Africa*, © 1934 by Lord Dunsany, published by Longmans Green & Co.

P. Schuyler Miller—"Ship-in-a-Bottle" by P. Schuyler Miller. Copyright 1944 by P. Schuyler Miller. First published in *Weird Tales*, January, 1945.

Hugh Noyes—"Forty Singing Seamen" by Alfred Noyes.

Mrs. William Outerson—"Fire in the Galley Stove." Copyright 1937 by Captain William Outerson.

The Society of Authors and Dr. Masefield O.M.—"Anty Bligh" from *A Tarpaulin Muster* by John Masefield.

Contents

Introduction

A few months ago, as I was working on this book, two ships collided in the fog outside New York Harbor. One was cut in half, with a substantial loss of life. Both ships were equipped with modern navigational equipment, including radar. Yet—they collided. Why? As this is written, the reason is still a mystery.

Just during the time I have been gathering the stories in this volume, the sea has provided other, even more dramatic mysteries. A freighter laden with sulphur vanished. No word of her fate went out over her modern radio equipment. She simply disappeared from sight.

And the U.S. nuclear submarine *Thresher,* new, one of the prides of the U.S. Navy, went down for a dive—and never came up. Why? We can make guesses as to what happened to her and the freighter, but all that can be said with confidence is that the sea took them, as it has taken countless thousands of vessels since the first man ventured out onto salt water in a crude canoe.

Because the sea is dangerous, unpredictable, and vast, and was for centuries a realm of mystery, it has always inspired stories of the strange and wonderful—unknown lands, terrifying monsters, phantom ships and ghostly spirits. We have found and charted all the unknown lands—or think we have—but the monsters may yet be found in the dark, ocean depths that we have not explored.

As for phantom ships and ghostly spirits, they are not hard to believe in for anyone who has witnessed the ocean in all its grandeur, power and terror from the deck of a ship in a great storm, or who has seen the soundless flame of St. Elmo's fire burning from the tips of masts or funnels.

In any case, the ghosts, monsters and wonders of the sea make fascinating reading for those of us who spend our lives on shore, safe from the perils of the deep. I hope you will enjoy these stories and poems as much as I have.

Robert Arthur
Cape May, N.J., 1965

DAVY JONES'
HAUNTED LOCKER

When young Jabez O'Brien found himself in Davy Jones'
Locker, it was a matter of some perplexity for all concerned.

Jabez O'Brien and Davy Jones' Locker

ROBERT ARTHUR

Some people will say that this story should start with Jabez O'Brien rowing his dory at midnight, oars muffled, into that patch of fog to meet the most wondrous adventure ever to befall a seagoing man. But if the story starts there, how are you to know who Jabez O'Brien was, and what he was up to, anyway?

No, it isn't practical. So, begging your pardon, I'll start with Jabez himself and work up to the adventure in its own good time.

Jabez O'Brien was a fisherman born. His father and his father's father before him had been fishermen, and so on back as long as there had been O'Briens. And as long as there had been fish, like as not.

The Jabez part of him was solid, rock-ribbed New England, practical and industrious. But the O'Brien side of him was Irish.

3

And at Jabez' birth on Fish Island, which lies off the coast of Maine, some passing spirit with a sense of mischief must have been present. Perhaps it was a leprechaun, blown off course and seeking passage back to Ireland. Whatever it was, it gave Jabez the soul of a dreamer.

The result was that as he grew up, the Jabez part and the O'Brien part of him just didn't pull oar together. On the sea of life Jabez went first one way, then the other, and looked likely to wind up no place.

When he put his mind to it, young Jabez was a welcome hand on any fishing boat in New England waters. The trouble was, just as the Jabez part of him started to get somewhere in the world—such as owning his own boat—the O'Brien part of him would issue different orders. Then he'd start woolgathering and daydreaming and let his boat wreck itself on a reef and almost drown himself. Which happened once and didn't happen twice because he couldn't save enough for another boat.

When Jabez daydreamed, it was about quite various matters. Sometimes he imagined that he was wise and famous. Sometimes he thought how nice it would be to be wealthy and happy. Sometimes he daydreamed he was all four things at the same time. Which just shows you how impractical he could be when he tried.

Mostly, though, young Jabez daydreamed of things nautical, the older the better. It seemed to him that in this twentieth century, though the sea was still large, mysterious, and dangerous, too much romance had gone out of life. Jabez couldn't help sighing over the days when the fabulous Sir Francis Drake became the first Englishman to sail around the whole world, and then later helped whip the mighty Spanish Armada when it came to invade England in the year 1588.

Then there was Captain Cook, another mighty navigator, who discovered much territory in the younger days of the world. Though of course he did get himself killed and eaten by cannibals on his last voyage.

4

Oh, the old days were glorious times in Jabez O'Brien's imagination. Many's the day when, all inside his own mind, he sailed into the unknown with Cook, fought Spaniards with Drake, or looted gold-laden convoys with the notorious pirate, Blackbeard.

But the result was—— Well, you can imagine it easily when I tell you that the town where Jabez lived was called Fishtown by its inhabitants, just as the island was called Fish Island. I'm speaking now of the names used by the natives who lived there, not the names on the map used by the summer visitors.

You can see that folk who called their town Fishtown and their island Fish Island would not have much regard for daydreams about the past. So, tall and broad-shouldered though he was, their attitude toward Jabez O'Brien was a little pitying, as toward one afflicted with an unfortunate handicap.

Even the girls of Fish Island shared this feeling, despite his merry eyes and curly black hair. For girls, and this is a secret I'm telling you, are very practical creatures for all their dainty looks. At least the Fish Island girls were. And they were of no mind to walk to the altar with someone who, like as not, would start daydreaming while his boat wrecked itself and he drowned himself, leaving them with no man in the house.

Jabez found this out when he proposed first to Susan Chavez, the most beautiful girl on the island. Susan said no, quite promptly.

Then he proposed to Nancy Lamb, the second most beautiful girl on the island. And Nancy said no also, though she made him wait a bit.

Finally he proposed to Maria Wellman, the third most beautiful girl on the island. And Maria also said no, though she made him wait the longest of all.

After this third rejection, Jabez did some hard thinking. There were other girls on Fish Island, but none of them took his fancy. He sometimes noticed that Nora Farrington, whose hair was reddish and who had a silvery laugh, was very easy to dip and whirl with when the Fisherman's Association held a dance in the recreation hall. But in his opinion her mouth was too wide and her eyes too far apart.

It was plain to Jabez that he must change the mind of Susan, or Nancy, or Maria. And to do this, he must change his station in life, become a man of importance on Fish Island. This he could do by becoming rich, which seemed impossible, or perhaps by becoming famous. Which seemed equally impossible.

Nevertheless, after long thought, Jabez decided on a plan of action.

He decided to catch a mermaid.

That would certainly make him famous, for no man had ever actually caught a mermaid before. And he could exhibit her to summer visitors and make a nice bit of change doing it. Then certainly Susan or Nancy, or at least Maria, would take a second thought and change her "no" to a "yes."

Jabez' plan was not as far-fetched as you may think. There was a cove on Fish Island where a mermaid was known to appear at certain intervals. True, no one had actually seen her, but daring seamen, most of them smugglers, had heard her singing in the night. And it is well known that mermaids have beautiful singing voices.

One grizzled old fisherman, José Sebastian, swore a solemn oath that he had not only heard the mermaid sing, but that she sang in Spanish. He had heard her one foggy night during Prohibition days when, as you may know, quite a bit of smuggling was done. At the time he had been landing some rare wines secretly in Mermaid Cove, as it was called. On hearing the singing he had left so promptly he had lost the entire cargo, which gave him a good memory for the year and night it happened.

So you can see why no one on Fish Island doubted that a mermaid really came to Mermaid Cove to sing. At least sometimes. Because the older fishermen had calculated, putting together all the reports they could come by, that she did not appear more than once every ten years.

Mermaid Cove was inaccessible and dangerous, even for smugglers. Landward, rugged cliffs made it almost unapproachable. Seaward, reefs made it impossible to enter in a small boat except at high tide. Sudden squalls blew up there on the slightest provocation and without notice. It was a good place to stay away from, and the men of Fish Island, being sensible, stayed away from it.

I'm not speaking of Jabez O'Brien now, of course.

Jabez had visited Mermaid Cove more than once. As a lad of thirteen, after climbing over the rugged cliffs in the darkness, he had actually heard song riding in from the cove on the ocean breeze one June night. Golden-voiced song such as José Sebastian swore to.

He hadn't been able to see the mermaid—it was too dark. But he had heard her. He knew she had been there.

Thinking back now with care, Jabez recalled that the night he heard the mermaid sing had been the night of his thirteenth birthday. He had received a thumping from his father for staying out so late, which had also helped fix the date in his mind.

Now a sudden idea came to Jabez. After a hurried visit to see old José Sebastian, he pulled some ancient nautical almanacs down from his shelves. With growing excitement he checked off certain dates. When he finished, he was breathing hard.

He had heard the mermaid sing just thirty years to the exact night after José Sebastian had. And putting together all the evidence, Jabez now felt quite certain that the mermaid appeared in Mermaid Cove only on the night of June 15th, in every tenth year.

But what made his pulse pound hardest was the realization that his own 23rd birthday came on June 15th, one week off. It would mark ten years exactly from the night on which he himself had first heard the song of the mermaid. According to all logic, she would be there again in a week, and if he were there also, with the proper kind of net, he could capture her. That was how simple it was.

(Now at this point I should tell you that Jabez' thinking was fine

7

and clear. He had indeed stumbled on something no one else had yet puzzled out. But not having full information he missed the truth of it by a trifle. The truth was even more wonderful than he thought. But to learn exactly what it was, read on.)

At all events, there Jabez was at midnight of June 15th, rowing into Mermaid Cove in a borrowed dory by the light of a three-quarter moon. On the seat beside him was a large net which he mended with nylon fish line until it was strong enough to hold a walrus, much less a delicate mermaid. His oars were muffled, he breathed softly, and he rowed with utmost quiet toward a large patch of fog which sat, most suspiciously, just in the middle of the calm water of the cove.

As he came near it, he heard song. A woman's voice—or a mermaid's—soared from the patch of fog. Jabez gave the dory a last pull and scrambled up into the bow, taking the net in his hand.

Then the dory slid into the fog itself, and Jabez' eyes came close to popping from his head. For inside the patch of fog the moon showed, not a mermaid seated on a rock, but a vessel peacefully at anchor. And the vessel was a Spanish galleon of a type that he knew had not sailed the seas for three centuries or more.

Yet there it rode, sails furled, all in darkness, the sound of a woman singing coming down to him from the broad windows of the captain's cabin at the stern. And beneath the sound of song he heard other voices, men's voices, murmuring, together with a clicking sound he could have sworn was the roll of dice on a wooden deck.

Jabez, forgetting what he had come for, gave a cry of astonishment. Then his dory hit the side of the great Spanish galleon. He expected a violent shock but instead the dory went right into the anchored ship as if it had been made of—well, not quite of mist, but perhaps of whipped cream.

In another moment Jabez O'Brien, his mind spinning, was inside the ship, in among holds and cabins, getting fleeting glimpses of Spanish sailors eating and drinking and making merry. And then as if his cry had been a signal, the ship was sinking spang on top of him, plummeting toward the bottom, pressing him down as it went even though he slid through it in a most peculiar manner.

Jabez suddenly found himself and his dory in the captain's cabin itself, being stared at by a Spanish grandee in full finery with a wine glass in his hand. A gentleman in the garb of an English naval officer of some centuries ago stood beside him, also holding a glass. And a beautiful young woman, whose long black hair was held in place by a jeweled comb, broke off singing to look at Jabez in astonishment and reproach.

In that moment Jabez at last realized the truth. There was no mermaid. He had heard a ghost singing. For the young lady and the captain and the ship itself could only be ghostly forms resurrected from ancient times. Then, before he could think further, his dory went under water. He went under with it. Being in the act of taking in a deep breath of astonishment, he took in water instead. And as the sea sucked him down, all went black in his mind.

When at last Jabez O'Brien opened his eyes a trifle, he said exactly what you or I would have.

"Where am I?" he asked.

"Ho!" a great voice roared. "Ho, ho!"

Jabez opened his eyes wide. Standing beside him was a somewhat odd individual, a full eight feet tall, with shoulders like the limbs of an oak and legs as sturdy as the mainmast of a sailing ship. His eyes were the green of the sea where it is shallow and his hair the blue of the ocean where it goes down to unplumbed depths. He wore only canvas trousers, hitched around his waist with a live eel.

Across the massive chest of the individual laughing at him, Jabez saw tattooed an American flag. As the fellow chuckled, his chest muscles rippled so that Old Glory seemed to be snapping in a half gale.

"Why, lad," the huge fellow said, "you're in Davy Jones' locker. And I'm Davy Jones, at your service."

9

"To speak the truth," Jabez said, sitting up, "that's what I was afraid of. I knew I'd meet you some day, sir, but I hoped it wouldn't be so soon. No offense intended."

"And none taken," said Davy Jones, his laughter ceasing. "To be accurate about it, Jabez O'Brien, you've arrived too early. Sixty-five years, four months, three weeks and one day too early."

"I never was good at keeping to a schedule," said Jabez. "Well, at least you're American. That's some consolation."

"Why, Jabez," said Davy Jones, "I'm not American. I'm not English or French or Russian or Spanish or anything else. I'm Ocean, and have been since the first man went out on salt water in a hollow log.

"I'm the Keeper of the Locker, and I receive all those who drown at sea. In order to make the shock a bit less, every man sees me as he thinks of me. If you were a Viking of the old days, you'd be seeing me with a horned helmet on my head and a wolfskin around my waist."

"Have I drowned then?" Jabez asked, with a natural curiosity.

He looked around him with interest, for he did not feel drowned, not by many a nautical mile. The room he was in had a rounded dome of a roof many feet above his head. As Jabez' eyes became adjusted, he saw that the room was a grotto in natural rock, its walls decorated with pearls by the million, some as big as his fist. The light came from even larger pearls, big as bowling balls, spaced here and there, each one with a glowing, phosphorescent jellyfish on it to give off illumination. And the huge bed he sat on might have been made of silk-smooth seaweed or of rare draperies too long underwater.

Without asking, Jabez knew it must be Davy Jones' own personal bedroom.

"Have you drowned?" Davy repeated his words. "Now that's a good question, a very good question. And right at the moment I'm not prepared to say."

"Then I'm alive?" Jabez asked, springing to his feet.

10

"Hold on!" roared Davy Jones. "I didn't say that. But if you're dead you're here sixty-five years too soon, and if you're alive you shouldn't be here at all. This is a very tricky case, young Jabez O'Brien, and it will take a bit of studying on my part.

"Why," he asked, with such a sigh that he blew out a dozen jellyfish, "did you ever have to sail smack into the ghost of the Spanish galleon *Princessa*? And indeed, right into the cabin of my good friend Don Alfredo Amandez, who went down with his ship and crew and beautiful daughter and English captive some three hundred years ago. Or was it four hundred?"

"Then that was a ghost ship!" Jabez exclaimed. "And it was a ghost girl singing. While all this time I thought it was a mermaid I was about to catch."

"Mermaids!" snorted Davy Jones. "They aren't in my department. Only ships that sink at sea and folks who go down with them or otherwise end up beneath the waters come under my jurisdiction. But when you got tangled up in the ghost of the *Princessa*, Don Alfredo didn't know what to do with you. So he pushed your dory free and brought you to me, seeing that he was coming here anyway, to join the Gathering."

"The Gathering?" Jabez asked, puzzled.

"Aye, the Hundred Year Gathering," Davy told him. "I see I shall have to tell you some things most men learn little by little while fish nibble on them. So here's the lay of the matter, and keep your ears open while I talk."

And indeed, what Davy Jones had to tell him took careful listening to understand, though when Davy finished, it seemed tolerably plain to Jabez.

When a ship went down at sea, it and all aboard came under Davy Jones' personal custody. The whole sea bottom was his locker, but this spot where Jabez was, of which Davy's bedroom was only the tiniest part, was a most tremendous hollowed-out harbor beneath a volcanic island, the center of his domain.

One night every ten years, the ghost of a sunken vessel might

11

rise again and the ghosts of its crew and passengers could enjoy a sight of the world above. For an hour they could do as they pleased, before returning to their rest in the waters that had claimed them.

Some several hundred years before, the Spanish ship *Princessa,* Don Alfredo Amandez captain, with his beautiful daughter and a treasure in gold aboard, had been blown far north of his course by a gale. Sighted by an English frigate, he had been engaged in battle. The two ships coming alongside, the crews fought savagely hand to hand until a sudden storm endangered both. The English ship had cast off and sailed away to England, leaving behind her captain, Sir Andrew Blade, seriously wounded. The *Princessa* had been blown onto the reefs of Mermaid Cove and sunk, on the night of June 15th in some year Davy Jones could not remember.

Since then her ghost had risen once every ten years, to lie at anchor in the cove while the ghostly crew yarned and feasted and diced. The ghostly Isabella, the captain's beautiful daughter, had used her hour to sing the songs that had soothed her father on the long voyage to the New World from which he had never returned. And it was this scene—Isabella singing, her father and Sir Andrew Blade listening as they drank wine—that Jabez had so rudely interrupted with his mermaid hunting.

"At least I was right that it happened but once every ten years, on my birthday night," Jabez commented. "But what I do not understand, Davy Jones, is why, if it was a ghost ship, I did not go straight on through her. For it is well known that ghosts are quite airy and have no more body to them than a bit of fog."

To this Davy answered that at sea ghosts take on a greater substance out of the water from which they come. This answer Jabez could understand. But he had still another question.

"This Gathering," he said. "You spoke of a Hundred Year Gathering. This is something I have never heard of before."

"Nor has any living mortal," Davy Jones answered. "Not," he added quickly, "that I'm admitting you are alive. You may just as well be drowned. I'm still studying the matter.

"But as to the Gathering. Once in every hundred years every last ship and every last man or woman or child who has been swallowed by the sea gathers here in the heart of my Locker for a frolic. Mayhap you have heard tell of Fiddler's Green, the seaman's paradise?"

Jabez nodded, and Davy continued, saying, "Fiddler's Green is really the Hundred Year Gathering. And the ghostly spirits of men and ships alike gather here for it. Now I've given you time and too much. Out you go to join the Gathering. Sir Andrew Blade will be your guide. Meantime I'll look into my books to see if you are dead, or alive, or quite possibly neither."

He turned to a shelf cut into the coral and took down a great, musty volume. As if at a signal the elegantly dressed Englishman Jabez had seen in the cabin of the ghost ship entered.

"Sir Andrew Blade, at your service," he said with a bow. Jabez responded in a like manner.

"Jabez O'Brien, who may be man or ghost or neither," he said. "If you are to be my guide, perhaps you can introduce me to Sir Francis Drake? And Captain James Cook, the great navigator, and Blackbeard, the equally great pirate? All of them are by way of being heroes to me.

"Although," he added, remembering, "Captain Cook died ashore, did he not? Landing in Hawaii he was slain, and then eaten by cannibals. So he can't be here."

Sir Andrew chuckled. "He's here. His bones were returned to the sea, so he wound up in Davy Jones' Locker after all. But come along."

With that he led Jabez forth. Outside, the young man found himself in a tremendous harbor formed, as Davy had said, beneath a volcanic island. He could not guess the size of the harbor, but it was crowded with craft of every kind, from every corner of the world and every moment of time.

Within eyesight he could spot Viking ships with carved dragon prows, Roman galleys, clipper ships from the China trade, battle-ships both old and new and, anchored close at hand, a great gash in her prow, a steamship.

He peered more closely and saw her name—*Titanic*.

"This way," said his guide. "Captain Cook keeps to himself. He's glum because he has no ship, being killed on land by the natives."

Sir Andrew led Jabez down a long wharf, and on all sides of him was merriment. Sailors roasted fish on spits, while others fiddled that some might dance jigs and hornpipes. Here and there were family groups picnicking placidly amidst the confusion. In the harbor was a constant coming and going of ships' boats of every description, and some Jabez had never heard tell of before.

What with ghostly spirits from a thousand lands and untold centuries of history making the most of their freedom this once in a hundred years, Jabez walked with his eyes wide and astonished. The whole cavern was filled with the greenish light, as of being under-water, which came from millions of phosphorescent jellyfish tucked here and there into the walls. And in some places electric eels were attached to chandeliers taken from sunken steamships, and were making them glow with great bursts of light.

Beneath one such patch of illumination, Jabez spied a group of English naval officers engaged in a game of ninepins on a smooth section of the wharf carved from coral.

"Sir Andrew!" he exclaimed. "Isn't that Sir Francis Drake himself? Knocking down ninepins, just as he did before he sailed out to smash the Spanish Armada in 1588?"

"That it is," said his guide. "And we'll see him next. Over here is Cook. We'll see if he feels like speaking to you."

He led Jabez toward a lonely figure, sitting apart from the merriment and staring glumly toward the harbor.

"A good day, Captain Cook," he called. "May I introduce to you young Jabez O'Brien, a visitor to the Gathering, an admirer of yours?"

14

Slowly, very slowly, Captain Cook turned. Jabez saw sharp eyes peer at him keenly from beneath bushy brows.

"He looks a likely seaman," Captain Cook said. "Irish, I take it?"

"Of Irish descent, sir," Jabez said politely. "We're from Maine now."

"Maine? The Spanish Main?" asked Cook, brows gathering together.

"No, sir. Down East Maine."

"I don't believe I've ever heard of it," Captain Cook said shortly. "I didn't make landfall on any Main save the Spanish one."

"It's one of the newer countries, Captain," Sir Andrew put in. "Only two hundred years old or thereabouts. Perhaps you'd care to tell our young friend something of your famed trips?"

"There's little to tell," and Cook sighed. "Last voyage, the ship sailed home. I didn't. Cook was the captain and the captain was cooked. Young man, let me give you some advice. Never let yourself be eaten by cannibals. You'll regret it as long as you live."

With that he turned and resumed his gloomy stare at a harbor which did not hold a ship for him to command. Sir Andrew nudged Jabez' elbow and led him away.

"He paid you a great compliment," he said. "He told you his favorite joke. Now let us speak to Drake. He's about finished with his game of bowls. In a few moments he'll be sailing out to attack the Spanish Armada."

"Attack the Armada!" Jabez exclaimed. "But he did that. Back in 1588 it was."

"Aye, and he'll do it again today," Sir Andrew said, leading Jabez toward a group of bowlers, who were applauding a throw in which Sir Francis Drake knocked down all nine of the pins.

"You see," he went on, "it's the big entertainment scheduled for this Gathering. For to a seaman a naval battle is what a mere game of baseball or cricket is to a landlubber. At each Gathering some great ocean battle is refought here in the heart of Davy

15

Jones' Locker. Afterwards, there is feasting and merrymaking. Aye, and dancing too, for we have many beautiful girls with us, though not as many as we sailors might wish."

"It's always been a dream of mine that I could have lived in the right age to fight with Drake against the Spaniards," Jabez O'Brien said. "At least, it will be a notable thing to see."

"As to that," said his guide, "perhaps Drake will give you a place on board one of his ships now. Some of them are shorthanded —not all the crews went to Davy Jones' Locker. We'll ask him."

Well, I could go on for a long time telling you of Jabez O'Brien's adventures during that Hundred Year Gathering in Davy Jones' Locker. For one thing, he fought aboard an English man of war which engaged two Spanish ships simultaneously. And though it was a ghostly battle, it was fought with great spirit, if you'll allow me the word, and much gunfire of a very realistic kind.

During the battle Jabez first was riddled by shot, then had his hand lopped off by a cutlass, and wound up with a cannonball going squarely through his midriff, as well as being mishandled in other serious ways. When the battle was over and he was allowed to reassemble himself, he was heartily glad it was only play-acting. He had lost all taste for warfare and never again daydreamed of the old times, or of pirates and sea fights.

Then came the partying, which he enjoyed a great deal more. Sir Andrew introduced him, formally this time, to the Lady Isabella, whose singing had created the legend of the mermaid in Mermaid Cove. The Lady Isabella, looking at him from beneath lowered lashes, chided him for so rudely interrupting her song. But she forgave him enough to dance with him.

Jabez would gladly have danced the entire night—or was it more than a night? for he could tell nothing of time—with the Lady Isabella. But from her arms he found himself whirled into those of other ghost girls whose fate had been to cast final anchor with Davy Jones. There were blonde Viking lasses, and dusky South Seas beauties, and dozens more, all eager to dance with him. For he was a

16

handsome stranger, and as Davy Jones had not yet decided about him, he was a deal less ghostly than the others present.

So time for Jabez O'Brien became confused entirely, and he could recall only whirling and dipping and spinning and whispering many sweet nothings into willing ears.

Then abruptly Davy Jones was standing beside him again, blowing on a great bos'un's whistle. In the twinkling of an eye the ghostly multitude gave over merrymaking and each individual returned to his ship. The ships themselves upped anchors and moved off, Roman galleys with oars dipping, sailing ships bending far over before some ghostly breeze, steamships bellowing forth black smoke.

In a second twinkling of an eye they were speeding toward some entrance so far off Jabez could not see it. In a moment, it seemed, they had sailed away and gone and there were only Davy and Jabez left.

"All ships and crews return to the spots where they sank," Davy said. "There to rest until the next Gathering. Save of course for the ten-year intervals when each can return to the surface for an hour to see the world above again. But you're still here, young Jabez, and to tell the truth, you're a thorny problem to me."

"I'm sorry to hear that," young Jabez answered. "It was never my intention to bother you, Davy Jones."

"I know, I know. You only wanted to capture a mermaid. Be that as it may, I've studied my books and my ledgers and I'm blowed if I can find a place to enter you. Dead or alive, you don't belong here and I'm sending you home again."

"Thank you, sir. Dead or alive, sir?"

"That's up to you, Jabez. I'm washing my hands of you. But this much I'll do. You've been put to considerable inconvenience, not altogether your own fault, so I'll grant you a wish before sending you off. If you wind up alive, you can use it. Contrarywise, at least I'll have done my best."

"That sounds fair," answered Jabez, already thinking hard what

17

to request, and planning how this turn of events might best be taken advantage of. Providing, of course, he could come out of the affair alive.

"So ask away, Jabez. Quickly. I have an appointment to meet a shipload of sailors just about to sign aboard with me up in the North Sea. What would you like?"

"Why," said Jabez, all in one breath, "I'd like to be richfamous- wiseandhappy."

By saying it very fast, as if it were all one word, he hoped it would count as a single wish.

"Ho!" Davy Jones bellowed. "Ho ho! Rich, famous, wise and happy, all at one and the same time. Jabez you rascal, even King Solomon couldn't manage all that. But——" and he clapped a great hand on the young man's shoulder, so that Jabez' knees buckled—"I'll do it. It so happens I've taken a liking to you."

"Thank you, sir," Jabez said.

"As to being rich," Davy told him, "you remember the rock in front of your little cottage, where you sit and look at the sea and daydream when you should be out doing some honest fishing?"

Jabez blushed slightly, but nodded.

"Under that rock are one hundred gold doubloons, hidden there by a survivor of the *Princessa* when she sank on the reefs of Mermaid Cove. They are just waiting for the rock to be overturned and found."

"No fisherman could ask for more wealth than that, sir," Jabez told him. "Being rich now I'll be able to marry the most beautiful girl on the island, or at least the second most beautiful. Or at the very worst the third most beautiful. Then I'll be happy. As for being wise and famous, I can let those go, I expect."

"Hold hard!" Davy Jones roared. "I'm not finished. I've given you wealth. If you get back alive, you'll be famous. Now to give you wisdom. Here it is. Don't marry the most beautiful girl on the island."

"Not marry Susan?" Jabez cried in astonishment. "Well then,

18

I'll marry Nancy."

"And here's the next round of wisdom. Don't marry the second most beautiful girl on the island."

"Not marry Nancy either?" Jabez exclaimed, in still greater amazement. "At least there's still Maria left."

"And here's the final wisdom. Don't marry the third most beautiful girl on the island."

"Not Susan, or Nancy, or even Maria?" Jabez said, very perplexed. "Excuse me for being bold and asking, Davy Jones, but where is the wisdom of that?"

"Why, Jabez," Davy told him, "the most beautiful girl on any island will spend her time being proud of her beauty and demanding that you notice it and give her trinkets to show it off. And when

age takes her beauty away, she'll most likely be miserable and make you miserable too."

"Hmm," said Jabez, who had noticed in Susan a certain fondness for pretty earrings and other such gadgets.

"And the second most beautiful girl will be rueful because she's not first. She'll ask for even more geegaws and trinkets. And as for the third most beautiful girl, she'll spend the most time of all in front of her mirror, doing things to her face and hair and trying to outshine the others. And she'll want even more pretties to make people notice her. Do you follow me, Jabez?"

Jabez did. It was indeed wisdom that Davy Jones spoke.

"Who then shall I marry?" he asked. "How can I hope to pick the right girl out of all the girls on the island? Polly has a sharp temper and Lettie talks too much and Sally——"

"The last bit of wisdom is this," said Davy. "Marry the girl who thinks you are the handsomest man on the island, the girl who thinks you are bravest and smartest and finest of all. Then you can be sure you're right. For she will spend her time thinking of you and not of herself. Now one last gift for free. You shall always be able to catch exactly the fish you need, no more, no less. But you must work to do it. So be off with you!"

He gave Jabez a thrust in the back with his tremendous hand, and Jabez went flying into the water. He struck hard and went down, down, and still down to a depth he could not calculate. At last he could hold his breath no longer and all consciousness of life left him.

But I am happy to be able to tell you this was not quite the end for Jabez O'Brien. It is true that he was seen to pop to the surface just off the beach of Fish Island, after being missing for ten mortal days. And his neighbors, having pulled him ashore, knew perfectly well that anyone who has been under water ten days must be buried. So they dug him a grave, put him in a coffin, carried him to the churchyard, and waited solemnly while the pastor said some final words over him.

Jabez, however, as he figured out later, had just been getting his breath back. For at that point he sat up. Seeing how matters lay, he hopped out of the coffin and refused to let himself be buried. He had to fight several of the men, who thought he was acting in an improper fashion, but when he had thrown three of them into the open grave they decided that he was still alive after all, just as he claimed.

In order that the occasion should not be wasted, what with everyone wearing his best clothes, Jabez O'Brien gave a party instead. He paid for it with one of the gold doubloons, found just where Davy Jones had said they'd be. And during the dancing first Susan, then Nancy, then Maria whispered to him that if he wanted to ask a certain question again, he'd get a different answer this time. But Jabez only looked wise and said nothing.

Nora Farrington, however, spoke differently. She confided to him how she had wept when his dory had been found, keel up, and him missing. And how glad she was that he was safe, he being the finest and handsomest man on the island. And suddenly Jabez noticed that her mouth was generously sized for laughter and kisses. And her green eyes were set well apart so that she could see the world clearly and still like what she saw. Her reddish hair, he perceived, was his favorite color.

So it was Nora he married. From that day on he worked hard at being a fisherman and he always caught fish in just the amount he needed. Nora took good care of his wealth, making sure it was not wasted. And Jabez was famous through all New England as the man who sat up in his coffin after being under water for ten days— for he said nothing about his meeting with Davy Jones, not wanting to be called a liar.

There are times now, it is true, when he wonders if it all really happened. He could test the matter by visiting Mermaid Cove on his birthday night, every tenth year, to hear the ghost of the Lady Isabella sing. But it so happens that with Nora and the children around, and the birthday party they give him, and one thing and another, that's one night he can never get away.

However, there's no denying that he has wealth, wisdom and fame, which make him believe that the visit to Davy Jones' Locker was indeed real. Sometimes it occurs to him that Davy did promise him happiness also, but at the last moment seemed to forget about it. However, he's willing to put that down as a mere oversight, what with Davy having so much on his mind.

The truth is that having married just the right kind of wife, and living exactly the life he wants to live, and having his work rewarded exactly right, with not too much and not too little to show for it, he's happier than any king who ever lived.

But happiness is a lot like breathing—when you really have it you don't notice it to think about. So if Jabez O'Brien doesn't give Davy Jones his full due it is only because he's human. And will be for a long time yet.

It was a strange sight for the Red Sea on a broiling hot day—
a sight so strange it belonged only in a nightmare.

One August in the Red Sea

LORD DUNSANY

As I came into the Club the other day they were talking of ele-
phants. Much more sagacious than dogs, they were saying. Well,
it doesn't really matter what they were saying, as none of it was
new, or even out of the ordinary. "But they remember an injury for
ages," said another of them. "Revengeful beasts," said another. And
gradually from then on, the elephant began to lose, so far as the
Billiards Club was concerned, his reputation for intellect, in ex-
change for one of long and revengeful brooding. And that is how
it would have been left but for Jorkens, and distinctly unfair to the
elephant. But Jorkens broke in on a tale of a long-brooded revenge
over some trifling matter of a bad orange with the words: "That's
nothing to men."

"Men?" we said, surprised at such a comparison.

"Yes," said Jorkens. "Nothing to the way they'll brood and revenge themselves."

We didn't think humanity was as petty as all that. Why, to be human means the very opposite of all that sort of thing. And so we said. And Jorkens, to prove his point, said: "I knew a man once, a Greek, who thought he was laughed at or slighted. And he planned for two years to fool the man who had made a fool of him, and at the end of that time he did it, and it must have cost him thousands and thousands. What do you think of that? Would an elephant spend all that time and money over such a trifle? No, it takes a man to be such a fool as that."

"But what did he do?" we asked.

"I'll tell you," said Jorkens.

And that's how I came to hear that singular story of August in the Red Sea.

"This Greek," said Jorkens, "was on a British liner going southwards down the coast, traveling on business. He was a glass manufacturer somewhere in Egypt, and he got on at Port Sudan. I imagine he made nearly all the tumblers and wine glasses in Egypt, and he was making that journey so as to extend his business to Durban and Capetown. I was only going to Durban myself. Well, we came to the line, and this Greek had never crossed it before. We had the usual game crossing the line, and the ship's officers took it all up very keenly and helped to make the fun go. Of course we had Neptune on board, with a fine beard made out of rope, and, well of course the joke's not very funny, so they did all they could to make it go, trying to amuse the passengers to make them forget the heat, and of course some got ducked in a swimming bath, which helped to cool them too. It wasn't that that seems to have irritated the Greek, but being told by the captain that this really was Neptune, just come out of the sea. Of course the captain was only trying to make it go; so as to amuse everybody. An elephant would have seen that much. But this Greek felt himself insulted by being treated, as he called it, like a child, because—as he said—he was a

26

foreigner. And of course that wasn't the reason at all, he was only selected because he had never crossed the line; it was his turn; and any fooling was only done to make the passengers forget the blistering heat. Anyhow he flared up. '*We* gave Neptune to the world,' he said, 'before the rest of Europe was civilized. We, the Greeks. And they think they can treat me like a child. Me, a Greek. *We* fooled the world with Neptune, before you were civilized.'

" 'Poseidon, wasn't it,' I said, to check his fury, for it was mounting higher and higher and I didn't know what he would do.

" 'Yes,' he shouted with the most triumphant scorn, 'and you could never even get the name right.'

"Well, after that I said no more. It doesn't sound much of a score, but from the way he shouted it he seemed to think he had vindicated Greece against the whole of Europe. I thought at first that that would have satisfied him, but not a bit of it. He went away and brooded; said no more for the rest of the voyage, and made his absurd and elaborate plans to be revenged on the captain by fooling him and his officers as they, as he put it, had tried to fool him.

"Well, I got off at Durban, and in two years' time I was on the same ship again. I used to knock about the East African coast a good deal in those days, going to one place and another. I was on the same ship going northwards, and at the very end of August we entered the Red Sea. Well, of course you know that can be a frightful experience. Two deserts lie like the sides of an oven, and the Red Sea is in between. Men not in the least emotional start at a point, in heat like that, when very little more is required to drive them clean crazy. And it was a particularly bad August, even for the Red Sea.

"Well, I was sitting on the deck about lunch time, and the rest were below having lunch. What on earth they wanted to have lunch for in that heat I can't imagine. I had the best kind of deck chair."

"What kind is that?" Terbut interrupted quite needlessly.

"There are only two kinds," said Jorkens; "the one with a hole to hold a tumbler in one of the arms of the chair; and the other kind has two holes. I was lying in my deck chair, when the captain came running up with a note in his hand that they'd evidently sent down from the bridge. He came out on the passengers' deck because it was the nearest deck to the dining saloon. We were just passing a rocky island. The captain went to the side and looked out ahead of the island. Then he put up his glasses, and when he took them down I distinctly saw tears in his eyes."

"Tears!" said Terbut.

"Yes," said Jorkens. "They were running down his face."

"Sweat," said Terbut.

"Sweat? Of course there was sweat," said Jorkens. "It was the Red Sea in August. But these were tears, and he went and sat down in one of the chairs and sobbed.

"I went to the side myself then and looked over, round the corner of that red island where the captain had looked; and about a mile from the island I saw what he had seen. I went straight to my cabin and lay down and kept quite quiet, and sent for the ship's doctor. I said: 'It's not my brain, doctor. It's my eyes. My brain's all right.'

"And he said: 'That's all right. I'll give you something for it.'

"And I said: 'Doctor, I'm not going to touch a drink all day. I'm going to do just what you tell me.'

"And he said: 'That's quite all right. I'll send you something by the steward, and don't get up till I see you again. It's very hot.'

"And I drank it when it came, and slept for twelve hours. And as soon as I woke I knew that everything was all right."

"Yes, yes," said Terbut, "but you tell us that you saw the captain of a British ship in tears?"

"It was the heat," said Jorkens. "I tell you it was at the end of August in the Red Sea, not thirty miles from the Gates of Hell, as they call them, and no straits are better named. It was that still, oven-like heat. And then suddenly seeing this, and thinking his reason had broken down, and his career ended; never another job for him at sea again; and a family, likely as not, brought to the brink

28

of starvation, at any rate all their leisure and comforts gone. He'd never have given way like that in England, or on any decent sea; but the heat there is perfectly frightful; and seeing a thing like that all of a sudden, when he was limp with the blazing heat."

"But what was it?" we shouted, for he really seemed to be rushing past the point.

"Well, of course it must have been some fake of that glass manufacturer," said Jorkens. "That Greek I told you of. He had no real competitors in the glass trade in the whole of that continent; so he could afford to do anything."

"Yes, yes, yes. But what *was* it?" asked Terbut.

"An iceberg," said Jorkens.

"An iceberg!" came from us all, quick as a cough.

"Yes," said Jorkens with an earnest sadness, "and what went to my heart in that frightful heat, and so far away from home, was a little patch of snow that it had on the top. Frosted glass, I dare say; but it went right to my heart."

The Three Fishers

CHARLES KINGSLEY

Three fishers went sailing down to the west,
   Away to the west as the sun went down;
Each thought of the woman who loved him the best,
   And the children stood watching them out of the town:
     For men must work, and women must weep,
     And there's little to earn, and many to keep,
Though the harbor bar be moaning.

Three wives sat up in the lighthouse tower,
   And trimmed the lamps as the sun went down;
And they looked at the squall, and they looked at the shower,
   While the night-rack came rolling up ragged and brown;
     But men must work, and women must weep,
     Though storms be sudden, and waters deep,
And the harbor bar be moaning.

Three corpses lay out on the shining sands,
   In the morning gleam as the tide went down,
And the women are weeping, and wringing their hands,
   For those who will never come home to the town.
     For men must work, and women must weep,
     And the sooner it's over, the sooner to sleep,
And good-bye to the bar and its moaning.

The galley stove was lit and the table was set, yet the ship sailed without a man aboard, living or dead.

Fire in the Galley Stove

WILLIAM OUTERSON

The ship *Unicorn* loitered to the westward, running large with a gentle breeze from the south. In the light of the brilliant moon her decks gleamed whitely; aloft, sly shadows played among her sails and spars. Overside, the quiet sea murmured as she passed.

Mister Mergam stood on the weather side of the poop, staring sourly ahead and seeing though not perceiving the beauty of the night. His keen ears caught the various sounds of ship and sea and wind, and his trained mind recognized them automatically, especially the soft thud of the rudder as the sea touched it, now on one side and now on the other. It was a simple sound, near and familiar, relentless as fate and sounding a note of caution, obscurely ominous, as if the voice of the helm attempted to warn him against any lack of vigilance. In this particular morning watch it gave him that impression, not because he was feeling down and defeated, since he had felt that way for years, but owing to his mood of sour rebellion, which had now reached a climax. He hated the empty plains of the sea and the narrow rounds of sailing-ship duties, but had to endure them because he could not make a living ashore.

Through all his years of roving, even on nights like this, he had remained blind to the beauty of the sea, and now his feeling toward it had settled into weary hatred. He knew its effects of blended color, its wide gradations of sound and action, the tireless charm of a sailing ship's effortless movement, the quality of silent distance and the wonder of the skies. Dimly at times, in moments of rare emotion, he had caught a glimpse of the mystic hand that beckons beyond the horizon and felt for a little while the fated urge of the wanderer. But that was in the beginning, long ago when he had first gone to sea, and he had forgotten it.

The lee side of the deck, to starboard, abounded in shadows cast by the moon. Under the mainsail a dark blotch extended from the half deck to the main hatch, and a bright space lay between that and the forward house. Observing this with his customary dull disinterest in details not requiring action, he watched the shadow thrown by the foot of the mainsail, backing and filling in the languid breeze. Raising his eyes from the deck to the sail, he suddenly stiffened and gazed unseeing in front of him as he felt an unusual movement of the hull, a strange shaking that startled him because it was outside of all his former experience. The whole ship, hull and spars and rigging, trembled eerily, and all the gear aloft made a weird clatter. He had never known any ship to move like this, and as he stood wondering what had caused it the skipper came hurriedly from the companionway and halted beside him.

"What was that?" he demanded nervously.

"I don't know, sir," Mister Mergam answered. "I've never felt anything like it until now, so I wouldn't know what it was."

"You don't know!" exclaimed the skipper. "You're here on deck in charge of the ship and something scrapes along her side—a derelict, more than likely—and you don't know what it was! You don't know." The skipper waved his hands helplessly. "Why don't you know? Didn't you see anything? Invisible things don't shake a ship like that. It must have been something big enough to be seen. Were you asleep?"

"No, sir, I wasn't asleep. I was wider awake than you are now, attending to my job, and I saw nothing. There was nothing to be seen. The lookout didn't see anything, or he would've reported it, and the man at the wheel didn't see anything, either."

"The man at the wheel," the skipper repeated unpleasantly. "How do you know he didn't see anything? It isn't his job to see things and report them. He's there to steer the ship, not to keep lookout."

The mate turned away sullenly and approached the man at the wheel.

"Did you see what shook her a minute ago, Thomson?" he inquired.

"No, sir," Thomson answered. "I didn't see nothin'. I looked astern after she stopped shakin' an' there wasn't nothin' in sight."

"You heard what he said, sir," Mister Mergam remarked to the skipper in a tone of meager triumph. "There was nothing in sight."

"Aye, I heard him," Captain Garton returned impatiently. "What do you suppose it could have been? Possibly a submerged derelict."

"No, sir, I don't think so. It wasn't the sort of shock any kind of a derelict would give. I've been in collision with a derelict, and it was something entirely different. This was strong, but soft and trembly. A derelict would grind and scrape along her side and make enough noise to wake the dead."

"I suppose you're right," the skipper admitted unwillingly. He moved away from the mate and stood with his hands on the poop rail staring at the sea ahead, a tall man, gaunt and irascible from chronic dyspepsia due to overeating and lack of exercise, tired of life and hating everybody, including himself. His excessively bright

35

eyes wandered fretfully along the deck on the weather side, which was lit by the moon except for an edge of shadow here and there, and he glanced at the leech of the mainsail. Something attracted his attention then, and he looked over on the port bow. A startled exclamation broke from him and he threw up his arm in swift apprehension, pointing urgently.

"Hey, Mister Mergam!" he cried. "What's that?"

The mate looked in the direction indicated by the captain's finger and noted a lifting of the skyline, an effect he had often observed while approaching a high coast from the sea, though this was not quite so well defined. He stared in silence and without understanding, disregarding the impatient questions of the captain until he arrived at the conclusion that the elevation ahead was a great wave approaching the ship at high speed. In the moonlight he could see its steep unbroken slope shining like bright metal and rushing toward them, and he was disturbed by the thought that it might sweep the decks clean.

"It's a big wave, sir," he said at last in faint excitement.

"Yes, it is," the skipper agreed. "It couldn't be anything else. And it explains the shaking of the ship a few minutes ago. There's been an upheaval of the sea bottom, a submarine earthquake, and when the sea bottom shook, the sea shook with it. The sea floor hereabouts has risen nearly two thousand feet during the past twenty years."

"Tidal wave on the port bow, sir," the lookout reported belatedly. He had been uncertain what name to give it, or whether to make any report about it, since waves of any size are not usually reported aboard ships at sea. They take them as they come.

"Aye, aye," replied Mister Mergam. "Close all ports forward."

They could see the forms of the men moving about on their bare feet as they carried out this order, scattering silently and passing among the shadows from the sails on the foremast. The ports were closed in a little while, and the men thought they ought to shut all the doors, but before they could begin to do this the big wave rolled up like the side of a mountain.

The skipper and the mate watched it come, not expecting any particular trouble from it, whatever its size, since ships are built to ride the seas in all weathers and conditions, and the wave was approaching from a favorable direction, about two points on the weather bow. As it drew nearer and revealed its enormous size, its smooth crest towering loftily above the level of the sea, the two officers began to feel doubtful. They could hardly expect the ship to ride dry over such a mass of water as that, so abruptly sloped and moving so swiftly.

When it reached the bows of the *Unicorn*, she gave a mighty heave and lifted her head in a gallant effort to climb the watery height, but she could not rise swiftly enough. Halfway up, her bow-sprit and cutwater drove into it, and broke over her, coming down on the decks with a solid crash that seemed to beat her under the sea. It swept over the forecastle head and rolled along the main deck in an avalanche, submerging the skipper, the mate, and the man at the wheel. They held on grimly, and in a few seconds the wave passed on.

The water sluiced off the decks into the calm sea, and soon all was normal again, save that the galley fire was out, the morning coffee was ruined, and all the pots and pans were adrift in eighteen inches of salt water. Both forecastles were flooded, because the watch on deck, having been given barely enough time to close the ports, had not been able to shut the doors, and the watch below came sputtering out, cursing the blokes for not having sense enough to do such things without waiting for orders.

"Call yourselves sailors," they sneered malevolently. "You ain't got sense enough to tighten your belts when your pants are slippin' down. Nurses is what you need." They raved back and forth till somebody struck out and the forward deck became a tumbled scene of fighting sailors, cursing and mauling each other but inflicting no serious injuries. Like a pack of sportive demons in the shadows of the moon they rolled about the main deck as far aft as the main hatch, locked in fierce embraces of sound and fury.

The skipper and the mate stood on the poop watching the brawl, and a light came into Mister Mergam's eye. Extracting a heavy teakwood belaying pin from the taffrail, he swung it gently up and down, almost lovingly, holding it loosely in his right hand.

"I'd better put a stop to that," he suggested to the skipper.

"No," said Captain Garton. "They won't hurt each other too much, and a little exercise will do them good. They've had it too easy this passage."

Mister Mergam seemed disappointed by this decision, but he obediently replaced the pin in the rail and continued to watch the waning battle on the forward deck.

Before long, the rage of the men abated and they separated two by two. Returning to their respective forecastles, they found that the water had drained out through the scupper holes, so the starboard watch lit their pipes and turned in to smoke while falling asleep. In the galley the cook cursed tidal waves and everything else as he gathered up his pots and pans and relit the fire in the stove after cleaning out the mess of sodden coals. It was now half-past four, and morning coffee—the most welcome event of the day to seafaring men—was due at two bells, therefore he must hurry. He would have a fresh brew ready in time if it could be done.

The skipper felt better after witnessing the fight between the watches, and he smiled for the first time in weeks as he listened to the reeking obscenities of the cook. There was something reckless and defiant in his piercing blasphemies that pleased the old man, who suffered a great deal from indigestion. But he soon became aware of the chill from his wet clothing and turned toward the companionway with a sigh.

"Keep a sharp lookout, Mister," he said to the mate as he started down to the cabin. "We don't want any more tidal waves."

"Very good, sir," Mister Mergam replied, swearing under his breath. The skipper's remark seemed to imply that he was to blame for tidal waves. "Old fool," he muttered. "He didn't even know the difference between a collision with a derelict and an earthquake shock."

In the port forecastle the men of the watch were changing into dry dungarees and discussing after their fashion the events of the morning.

"That was a big sea," said one.

"Aye, it was, but I've seen bigger off the Horn," old Charlie declared.

"You never seen a bigger one anywheres, Charlie. You must of dreamt it."

"This old hooker is full of bad luck."

"So she is. She ain't had a lucky day since we left port."

"When d'ya think coffee will be ready?"

"Ask the cook. Mebbe he knows."

"I give Snooky in the sta'bo'd watch a coupla black eyes."

"Take a squint at yer own."

"The skipper's crazy."

"Naw, he ain't crazy. He's sick. He oughta stay ashore."

"Say! Did ya feel that? What the devil was that?"

On the quiet poop Mister Mergam stood with feet apart, glancing listlessly at the skyline from time to time, casting his eyes aloft at the towering sails, surveying the deck, and watching the play of shadows born of the moon. The color of the sea had changed, and it no longer gleamed with the purple blue of deep water. As they were not within two hundred miles of the Grand Bank he surmised that the disturbance on the sea bottom had sent up clouds of ooze that imparted a dull hue to the water. While considering this, turning it over in his mind with slow interest, he felt the ship quiver again to a sudden shock, altogether different from the first. It felt as if a floating body, soft and enormously heavy, had come to rest against the bottom of the ship, and he went swiftly to the taffrail to peer intently over the side. At the same time he noticed the men of the watch running silently to the main rail forward, where they also stared down at the sea. Evidently they had felt the shock. The mate had just finished his casual observance of them when the skipper erupted on the poop again, very much annoyed.

"What was that, Mister Mergam?" he demanded in his usual exasperated tone. "That was no earthquake shock. Something hit her that time—you can't deny it. Something actual and material struck against her bottom."

"Yes, sir. I'm not denying it. Something certainly hit her then, and I'm looking to see what it was, but there's nothing in sight."

"Nothing in sight," the skipper repeated. "Nothing in sight. What in the name of all the mysteries is happening to this ship, anyhow? All sorts of things going on, and nobody knows anything about it!"

There came another soft, heavy shock, followed by others at short intervals.

"My God!" the skipper whispered, staring fearfully down at the muddy sea. More and more of the things, a whole crowd of them, monsters of some horrible sort, clamped along the ship's keel, driven up from the bottom of the sea by the disturbance down there! "What are they? Can you tell me that, Mister Mergam?"

"No, sir, I can't," the mate replied uneasily.

They stared at each other in the light of the sinking moon, two perturbed and bewildered men suspecting some lurking danger.

"The wheel's jammed, sir!" cried Thomson. "I can't move it."

The skipper and the mate turned and stared at the man, watching his strenuous but unavailing efforts to move the wheel.

"She's lost headway, sir," said Mister Mergam, looking over the side again. "She's standing still."

"You're right," the captain agreed in a different tone of voice, low and troubled. "These big brutes clinging to her bottom have stopped her, and one of them has clamped itself across the rudder. Whatever they are down there, they're keeping out of sight. Ah! There's another. That one struck forward under the bows. There must be a lot of them."

40

The man at the wheel, peering at the timepiece in the binnacle, saw that it was five o'clock. Forward on the forecastle head, the man on lookout struck the ship's bell twice, two measured strokes that boomed and lingered about the shadowy decks. Placid now, and smoking a short clay pipe as black as ebony, the cook, who had flaming red hair and hailed from Glasgow, thrust his head through the galley doorway and asked what the devil was wrong now. The men strung along the rail told him they didn't bloody well know what was wrong, but if he would hurry with the coffee they would tell him as soon as they found out.

"If there's anither tidal wave comin', give us a shout so's I can close the doorrs and the porrts," the cook requested.

"How about coffee?" they inquired, turning from the rail to observe him with the bantering regard that sailors bestow on sea cooks.

"It'll be ready in aboot ten meenits," he promised them.

In a little less time than that he beat with a ladle on the bottom of an empty pan, making a racket that might have been heard or felt by the beasts along the keel, and the men left the rail to fetch their hook-pots from the forecastle. They were puzzled and a trifle scared and had little to say to each other, though they had chattered enough when those queer shocks had been felt. Some of them thought whales had rubbed their backs against the hull, but others argued that this would not have stopped the ship's headway. There must be a lot of big soft beasts hanging on to her, scared up from the depths by the earthquake down there that had caused the tidal wave, or the ship wouldn't be standing still the way she was.

In silence they went one by one to the galley door and waited in line for their pots of coffee. Charlie was first. He stood at the door holding his hook-pot inside, to be filled with a ladleful of the stuff the cook called coffee, dipped from a boiler on the stove.

The skipper and the mate still waited at the taffrail for a sight of the things from the deep, and the long inaction had begun to affect their nerves.

"If we could only see them, and find out what they are," muttered the captain, "we might be able to decide on some plan of action. But how can we fight against invisible things of unknown nature!" He paced back and forth along a short path between the taffrail and the standard binnacle, frowning impatiently, clenching and opening his hands nervously.

Mister Mergam had glanced forward at the sound of the cook's gong, and he watched the men as they came out of the forecastle and went to the galley door to await their turn for coffee. The first man in line received his coffee and started for the fore hatch, where he intended to sit while drinking it. He did not see the long slender tentacle that quirted over the rail above his head and waved here and there seeking what it might find.

It found old Charlie as he reached the fore hatch, concealed from his watchmates by the corner of the forward house, wrapped itself around his neck with a strangling hold that prevented him from uttering a sound, and dragged him violently over the rail.

The next man, following with his coffee, saw Charlie at the rail, striking madly at the tentacle with his hook-pot, and a startled yell attracted the attention of the others. They spun around and saw old Charlie going over the side in a headlong dive with his waving hook-pot, but were too late to notice the deadly tentacle around his neck. They rushed to the rail and stared down at the dull water, but the man who had seen the tentacle held back. He knew the sort of beast it belonged to.

Men may sail the seas for a lifetime and seldom, if ever, come in contact with the nightmare monsters that inhabit the caves and cliffs of the ocean floor. Gazing down at the slightly muddy water, the men of the *Unicorn* saw a squirming mass of interwoven tentacles resembling enormous snakes, immensely thick and long and tapering at their free ends to the size of a man's thumb. It was a foul sight, an obscene growth from the dark places of the world, where incessant hunger is the driving force. At one place, down near the bulge of the hull, appeared a staring gorgon face with great lidless eyes and a huge parrot beak that moved slightly, opening and shutting as though it had just crunched and swallowed a meal of warm flesh. In its neighborhood the water was stained a reddish hue, possibly with blood from the veins of old Charlie. There were many of those deep-sea devils under the ship, ravenously hungry and now aware that there was food on her decks in the form of puny bodies that could be had for the taking.

Suddenly the men of the watch saw the air above the rail alive with tentacles. They swayed uncertainly for a second or two in order to feel the position of their prey, then lashed out with swift aim at the horrified men. Whipping round them, they tightened their hold to a vise-like grip that no human strength could break, though a sharp knife could slice them in two if properly used. The men were panic-stricken and struck wildly with sheath knives and hook-pots, but failed in their excitement to cut themselves off and went over the rail screaming. The boatswain, carpenter, and sail-maker jumped up from the main hatch and rushed across the deck to rescue the few survivors of the watch, but half a dozen tentacles seized them and jerked them over the side.

When the first tentacle came over the rail and fastened itself on Charlie, the steward was ambling forward to the galley for the cabin coffee. On seeing the man dragged violently over the rail the steward stopped and stared in amazement, trying to imagine what had happened to the sailor and thinking that perhaps he had become suddenly insane. The reeling gait of old Charlie, however, his struggles and the manner in which he went over the rail, convinced the steward that something had hold of him. His smooth-shaven face, round and placid, became puckered with anxiety and he stared in growing consternation at the struggle that developed between the men of the watch and the tapering tentacles that whipped over the rail in dozens. While he stood watching this primitive contest, a tentacle flung itself around his waist and dragged him down before his whimper could rise to a scream of terror.

The cook with the flaming hair came out of the galley with a carving knife and tried to run aft to the poop, but was caught. He slashed off the tentacle but was seized by others and dragged over, the severed tentacle clinging around his body. The men of the starboard watch tumbled out with drawn knives in ready hands. They had to divide forces to protect themselves on both sides, as the tentacles were now swaying above each rail from forecastle to poop. Though they fought with fury and some skill they had small chance to win against such desperate odds. Some of them jumped into the rigging to get out of reach by climbing aloft, but the men who tried that exposed themselves to the beasts lurking below and were snatched away immediately. There were too many tentacles to be cut, and even when they were slashed clean through they continued to cling around a man's body. They had suction cups on their under sides and rings of sharp claws within these.

"There's the answer," said the mate to the skipper when the battle began after the death of old Charlie. "The things sticking to the bottom are giant octopuses. They're the biggest things in the sea, except for the whales, and only the sperm whale can tackle them. He feeds on them, and sometimes they feed on him, if they can hold him down till he drowns. I'll get a knife and give the men a hand."

"Better do that than stand here telling me things I already know," the skipper retorted sharply. "There's men dying forward there."

The mate hurried to the companionway. He would go to his room for a hunting knife he kept there—a beautiful weapon hitherto useless, with an eight-inch blade as sharp as a razor. The octopus which had folded itself over the stern and jammed the rudder, aware that its companions were obtaining food from the top of this rocklike mass they were clinging to, flung two tentacles over the taffrail and waved one of them in Mister Mergam's direction.

44

"Look out, sir!" The man at the wheel screamed a warning.

Mister Mergam was just about to descend the companionway when he heard this cry. He threw a swift glance over his shoulder, saw the thing flicking toward him, and tried to jump down the companionway. He was too late. The tentacle wrapped itself around his chest and tightened. He strained against it, uttering a faint grunt, and braced himself with hands and feet against the hatch.

"Bring a knife, sir, and cut me loose," he implored the captain. The latter stared at him in horror and rushed away for a knife, going down the poop ladder to the door leading to the cabin from the main deck.

Another tentacle found the man at the wheel and caught him around the waist, binding one arm to his side but leaving the other free. It was the rule aboard the *Unicorn* that no seaman should wear a knife while standing his trick at the wheel, therefore Thomson carried none. He knew that human strength could not prevail against the power of these tentacles, though they could be cut, and he waited for the return of the skipper with the knife. Meantime, he made a sudden jerk and dragged the tentacle a couple of feet toward him, wrapped two turns of it around a spoke of the wheel, and held it fast there. It required desperate strength to do that with one hand, and he succeeded only because he was an exceptionally powerful man. Now the octopus could not drag him over the side without breaking the spoke, which was teakwood and very tough.

The mate had nothing but his hands, and these could not serve him. A sharp ax hung on the bulkhead a few steps below him in the companionway, and he made supreme efforts to go down there to secure this weapon. He was unsuccessful, for the octopus refused to slacken up and tightened its grip till the mate groaned with the pain of it.

Though the skipper had not been gone more than a few minutes, Mister Mergam thought he would never come back and cried in a gasping voice for him to hurry. Captain Garton shouted that he

45

could not find the knife in the mate's cabin and was bringing the ax from the bulkhead. He was coming right up.

"For God's sake, hurry!" the mate entreated. "The brute's crushing me."

The skipper wrenched the ax out of the slings and staggered up the companionway to cut Mister Mergam free, but as he reached him the mate was dragged violently away from the hatch. Captain Garton followed in urgent pursuit. Dashing out on deck, he made a swift step toward the unfortunate mate and swung the ax for a severing stroke, but before the blade fell Mister Mergam was whipped with a crash against the taffrail and went down over the side.

The man at the wheel found it difficult to hold against the pull of the octopus, even with a double turn of the tentacle around the spoke. He was gasping and purple in the face, and the harder he strove against it the tighter the tentacle was drawn. He was rapidly becoming exhausted.

After peering over the side for a few precious seconds to see what had become of his lost mate, the skipper drew back from the rail horrified and trembling. He was not a strong man. Turning toward the wheel, he noted the perilous plight of the man there, and stumbled across the deck intending to sever the tentacle where it was wrapped around the spoke. In his condition of quaking repulsion he could hardly lift the ax and stood for seconds trying to swing it above his head.

The octopus jamming the rudder eased its pressure down there, and the wheel spun around under the pull of the tentacle, which slipped off the spoke. Thomson was hurtled across the poop and over the side, crashing against the skipper and knocking him down. The ax fell from Captain Garton's hands, and he rose staggering to pick it up. As he seized it he saw another tentacle whipping over the rail toward him, and in a surge of blind fury he swung the ax, which left his hands and went flashing into the sea. He swooned when the tentacle gripped him, and the octopus drew him down.

Cowering on the forecastle head, the man on lookout saw the last of the crew go down to feed the octopuses, and his mind roved in every direction searching for a means of saving his own life. Up to the present no tentacles had come up over the head rail, and he stood absolutely still, hoping that they would not find him.

But in this he was disappointed. One of them came up and waved about, drawing nearer every second. Out of his mind with terror, the lookout sprang to the rail and saw in the water below the appalling face of an octopus. Taking his knife by the blade, he threw it with miraculous aim and saw it sink out of sight in the eye of the beast, which went into a tremendous flurry. Looking aft, the man saw that there were few tentacles now waving over the main deck, and he crept down the ladder to look for a knife. Stealing along the port side, he searched eagerly but could not find one, returned along the starboard side, and met the same result. All the men had gone down fighting with the knives and the hook-pots in their hands. Reaching the fore hatch, he decided to enter the forecastle and shut the door. The ports were already closed. But he was just a moment too late. They got him.

A little while later a pod of sperm whales came up to blow not far from the *Unicorn*; and the octopuses, feeling the near presence of their deadly enemies, went away from there and returned to the deep places.

The ship *Merivale,* heading eastward some days out of New York, sighted a ship with all sail set. She was observed to behave in an erratic manner and appeared to be abandoned, since there was nobody at the wheel or about the decks. In the gentle breeze that was blowing shortly after sunrise the strange vessel bore away to the west, came up in the wind with all her canvas flapping, paid off slowly, and bore away again, repeating this endlessly. The skipper and the second mate of the *Merivale* watched her queer behavior from the poop, and, as no answer was made to their signals, a boat was sent off to the stranger to investigate.

The boat pulled alongside the *Unicorn,* and the second mate was boosted to the rail. They hove up the boat's painter, which he made fast, and scrambled up beside him. Except for some stains of coffee on the foredeck, which had not completely dried, the decks were clear and shipshape. In the cabin the second mate noted that the table was set for coffee, but the dishes had not been used. He scratched his head in complete bewilderment. All the boats were in the chocks, their covers untouched, and there was no sign of disease or mutiny. As he stood pondering the mysterious situation, one of his men came aft and halted in front of him.

"They ain't been gone very long, sir," he reported. "The fire's still fresh in the galley stove."

There is an odd magic about those little ships in tightly sealed bottles. But about this ship and this bottle there was a stranger magic by far.

Ship-in-a-Bottle

P. SCHUYLER MILLER

I remembered the place at once.

I was nearly ten when I first saw it. I was with my father, on one of our exploring trips into the old part of town, down by the river. In his own boyhood it had still been a respectable if run-down district of small shops and rickety old frame houses. He had worked there for a ship chandler until he had money enough to go to college, and on our rambles we would often meet old men and draggled, slatternly women who remembered him. Many is the Saturday afternoon I have spent in the dark corner of some fly-blown bar, a violently colored soft drink untouched in the thick mug before me, while I listened to the entrancing flow of memories these strange acquaintances could draw up out of my father's past.

It was on one of these excursions, shortly before my tenth birthday, that we came upon a street which even he had never seen before. It was little more than a slit between two crumbling warehouses, with a dim gas lamp halfway down its crooked length. It came out, as we discovered, near the end of the alley which runs behind the Portuguese section along Walnut Street. One side was a solid brick wall, warehouse joined to warehouse for perhaps a hundred yards. On the other was a narrow sidewalk of cracked flagstones, and the windows of a row of shabby shops, most of them empty.

We might have passed it, for we were on our way to the little triangular plot of grass under the old chestnut, where Grand and Beekman come down to the river, and the chess players meet to squabble amicably over their pipes and their beer of a Saturday night. But as we passed its river end the lamp came on, and its sudden glow in the depths of that black crevice caught my eye. I pulled at my father's coat, and we stopped to look. I wonder now, sometimes, how and by whom that lamp was lit.

The shop door was directly under the light. We might not have seen it otherwise, although I have a feeling it was meant to be seen. Even in the dark it would have had a way of standing out. The flags in front of its door were clean, and the little square panes in its low front window shone. It had a scrubbed look, which grew even more apparent as we hurried toward it past the broken stoops and dingy plate glass of its neighbors.

It was my discovery, and by the rules of the game I was the first to open the door. But I stopped first to look at it, for it was a strange place to find in those surroundings. The street was old, but most of the buildings dated from the turn of the century, before the warehouses had gone up. They had the seedy straightness of the mauve era, corrupted now by the dry rot of poverty and neglect, but this place had a jolly brown look about it that went straight back into my picture-memories of Dickens' London. It was like the stern of a galleon crowded between grimy barges. Its window, as I have said, was low and wide with many little square panes of heavy greenish

52

glass set in lead. The flagstones in front of it were spotless, and the granite curbing with its carved numerals and even the cobbles out to the center of the lane had been scrubbed until they shone.

That, as we saw it first, was Number 52 Manderly Lane.

The street lamp shone down on its doorstep, but a warmer, mellower light was shining through the wavery old glass of its queer window. I think it was the first oil light that I had ever seen. I know I pressed my nose against the clearest of the little panes to peer inside before I opened the great oaken door. And what I saw was enchantment.

In the four years since my mother died and my aunt came to live with us, I had sat with my father in many a grimy little shop on these squalid back streets, and their dirt and stench and meanness no longer concerned me. I had come to expect it and to understand it. It was a part of the setting in which these pinched and tired people lived out their lives. A few of them had come up in the world, as he had, chiefly through political maneuvering or other even more questionable methods, but not many of them had lost the lean, wolfish look of hunger and suspicion which had become a part of them, ingrained as children and nurtured in youth. Those who had it least were among my father's warmest friends.

But this place was different. That was faery. It was the Old Curiosity Shop—it was the shop of Stockton's Magic Egg—it was all the wonderful places I had found in the dark old books in my father's library, rolled up into one and brought alive. It was deep, and broader than seemed possible from outside, with a wide oak counter running from front to back along the left-hand side. A great dim tapestry, full of rich color and magic life, hung on the right-hand wall next to the door.

The floor was of wide pine planks, sanded white. The ceiling was low and ribbed with heavy beams. And the scent of pine and oak were part of the wonderful rich odor which welled up around me as I opened the big door and stepped inside.

It was a faery odor as the shop was a faery shop. It had all the

53

spices of the Orient in it, and sandalwood, and myrrh. It had mint and thyme and lavender. It had worn leather and burnished copper, and the sharp, clean smell of bright steel. It had things a boy of nine could remember only from his dreams.

Behind the broad counter were cupboards with small-paned glass doors through which I could dimly make out more wonders than were heaped upon the worn red oak. Three ship's lamps hung from the ceiling, and their yellow light and the light of a thick candle which stood in a huge hammered iron stick on the counter, were all that lighted the place. Their mellow glow flowed over the sleek bales of heavy silk and swatches of brocade and crimson velvet, picking out the fantastic patterns of deep-piled carpets heaped against the wall under the tapestry, and caressing the smooth curves of gloriously shaped porcelains in ox-blood and deep jade. They half hid, half showed me the infinite marvels of an intricately carven screen in ebony and ivory which closed off the rear of the store, and the grotesque drollery of the figures on a massive chest which stood before it, of a family of trollish marionettes dangling against it, and of a set of chessmen which stood, set out for play, on a little taboret of inlay and enamel.

These chessmen my father saw, and went to them at once while I was still moving in sheer wonder from one thing to another, drawing the scent of the place into my lungs, letting my hungry fingers stay over all the strangeness spread out for their enchantment. The men were of ivory, black and red, and of Persian workmanship. I have them yet, and men who should know say that they are very old and fine.

Have I said that as I pushed open the great door a silver bell tinkled somewhere in the depths of the shop? I forgot it at once in the marvels of the place, so it was with a thrill almost of panic that I realized that the proprietor was watching us.

I don't know what I had imagined he would be like. A wizened dwarf, perhaps, wracked over with the years and full of memories. Or a bearded gnome of a man as jolly as his shop front and as full of sly magic as its interior. We read much the same sort of thing then that children do now, although my taste in melodrama may have been a bit old-fashioned.

Instead this was a huge man, a brown man with the puckered line of an old scar slashing across his throat and cheek, a man weathered by sea and wind, who would make two of my father and have room enough left for a boy as big as myself. He was of uncertain age—not old certainly, for his shock of hair was wiry and black, and not young either—and dressed in sun-bleached clothes with a pair of rope sandals on his bare feet.

My father looked him over, sizing him up as I had seen him gauge other strangers in these parts before opening conversation. He was satisfied, apparently, for he inquired the price of the chessmen and in doing so brought another surprise.

I suppose that I expected a rolling bass from so big a man—a man so obviously a sailor, and one who from his bearing had been an officer, accustomed to bellowing his commands above the roar of wind and sea. But it was small and soft and rasping, as if he had swallowed it and could not bring it up again. It made my backbone creep.

"They are not for sale," he whispered.

I had heard that gambit used before, and was rather surprised when my father did not follow it up in the traditional way, but turned instead to survey the contents of the counter and the shelves behind it. The shopkeeper lifted the iron candlestick and followed as my father stooped to examine a curious footstool made from an elephant's foot, or fingered a creamy bit of lace.

"The boy has a birthday soon," my father said casually. I was listening, you may be sure, with all my ears. "Perhaps you have something that he'll like."

The man looked at me. He had black eyes—hard eyes, like some of the bits of carved stone on his shelves. His face was cut by hard lines that made deep-bitten gutters from his hooked nose to the corners of his wide, cruel mouth. But his voice was as soft and rustling as his own fine silk.

"Let him look for himself," he said. "Here's a candle for him. And while he looks I'll play you for the men."

If my father was startled, he never showed it. He had learned control of his face and tongue as he had been taught control of his quick, hard body, of necessity and long ago in these very streets. "Good," he said, and drew from his vest pocket the gold piece he carried for luck. It was a Greek coin, I think, or even older. "Call for white."

The coin spun in the lamplight, and I heard the man's half-whisper: "Heads." It fell on the wooden floor, and my father let him pick it up. "Heads," the proprietor said softly, "but I have a liking for the black."

They drew up chairs beside the little table, and I on my part soon forgot them in the wonders which the candlelight revealed. I stood for a long time, I remember, examining the tapestry which stretched all the length of the farther wall—its fabric darkened by age, but full of life and color depicting a history of a mythology which I could not and still cannot place. I grew tired of it, and had a moment's fright as I caught the empty eyes of a row of leering masks watching me from the rafters above it. Then I turned back to the clutter on the long counter and began to rummage through it for whatever I might find. The cupboards tempted me, but it was with a queer sensation that I heard the proprietor's husky voice: "Go on, boy—open them."

It was a long game, I think. I was so full of the strangeness of everything, and so desirous of making exactly the right choice in all that mass of untold wonders, that I might never in my life have decided what thing I wanted most. And then I found the ship.

I am sure now it was chance—pure chance—or if it was fate, a fate more far-reaching than anything we know. I had opened cupboard after cupboard, holding the heavy candlestick high to see or setting it down on the counter behind me to fondle and explore. There were deep drawers under the cupboards, and more under the counter, and I hunted through those, finding new wonders every moment—trays in which gaudy butterflies had been inlaid in tropic woods, trinkets of gold so soft and fine that I could scar it with my nail, jewels of a hundred sorts, and the mummies of strange small animals. One cupboard seemed to stick, and when I pulled it open the whole wall came with it, leaving a paneled niche almost five feet deep. In it, set in an iron cradle, was a great glass bottle—a perfect sphere of thin green glass—and in it was the ship.

It was an old ship, a square-rigger, perfect in every detail. Most ship models that I had seen in the waterfront shops were small and rather crude, stuffed into rum bottles or casual flasks which had happened to come the maker's way, with more ingenuity than pride of craftsmanship. This ship was different. Where the routine ship-in-a-bottle bowled along under full sail, heeling a bit with the force of the imaginary gale that stretched its starched or varnished canvas, this ship lay becalmed with her sails slack and the sun beating down on her naked decks. There was not a ripple in the glassy sea in which she lay. The tiny figures of seamen, no bigger than the nail of my little finger, stood morosely at their tasks, and on the bridge a midget captain stared up at me and shook in my face a threatening arm which ended in a tiny, shining hook.

I knew then that I wanted that ship more than I had ever wanted anything in all my life before. It wasn't the flawless craftsmanship of the thing, or the cunning art which had sealed it within that seemingly flawless globe of glass. It was because—and I say this after thirty years—it was because I had deep in my child's soul the conviction that this ship was somehow real, that she sailed somewhere in a real sea, and that if only she were mine I could somehow find a way of getting aboard her and sailing away to adventures beyond the dreams of any boy in all the world.

I turned to call my father. The game was over, and he stood, an oddly thoughtful expression on his lean face, staring down at the final pattern of men. For he had won. The chessmen were his. But the shopkeeper was looking not at him but at me, and although the light was behind him I did not like at all what I thought was in his face.

I stepped quickly backward. The candle tilted and hot grease splashed my wrist. I think my elbow hit the open cupboard door as I jerked it back, for I felt it give and heard it close. Then with tiger-ish speed the brown man was across the shop, leaning across the counter. He pulled it open—and there was no ship there.

I thought there was a threat in his strange hushed voice. "Well, boy," he whispered, "your father's beaten me. What do you want?"

I set the candle down between us and backed away. I wanted nothing more at that moment than to get out into the street again, where there were lights and people and my father. All the wonder of the place was swept away in an emotion that was as much guilt as fear, as though I had pried into forbidden things—for that was in his voice.

"N-nothing, sir!" I told him. "Nothing at all."

"Nothing?" It was my father. "Nonsense, Tom. Don't be a fool. This is a wonderful place. I've done this gentleman out of some very valuable chessmen, and we must give him his chance at us. Now—what do you want?"

It was queer how his being there changed everything. There was no more fear and there was no reason at all for feeling guilty. A kind of defiance grew up in me in their stead, and I looked straight into those hard black eyes and answered.

"I'd like a ship, I think—a ship in a bottle."

That's almost all, except that I got a ship. I had asked for one, and my father, feeling rather odd at having won so valuable a prize, insisted that I choose. I made a long business of it, hunting all the shelves and through all the cupboards, and at last I chose a frigate that I realize now was a masterpiece for all its lifeless, straining sails and plaster wake. But there was no becalmed clipper with sun-drenched crew, hung in a green bubble as broad as my arms could span. And for a good many years, after we had moved to another town and I had found a new school and new friends, and eventually

58

work, I wondered why . . .

I knew the street at once when I saw it again.

I had been looking for it, as a matter of fact—not actively, but in a casual sort of way as I walked the old streets along which I had trotted with my father thirty years before. They still played chess of a summer night in the little park where Beekman meets the river, but the players I had known were gone. People in those parts do not forget so easily, though, and I talked of old times and agreed that the new ones were decadent and drab. It was near midnight of a glorious night full of stars, so I turned naturally to the river front and strolled along the empty street with only my shadow for company, listening to the slow echo of my footsteps and thinking of nothing at all but the night.

The street lamp threw a band of light across my way, a little brighter than the starlight. At the same moment I stepped down from the curb and felt uneven cobbles underfoot, and somehow the two combined to break through my revery and bring a memory up through the veil of years. I looked up, and it was there.

In thirty years the lane had grown dingier and darker, and the patch of scrubbed flagging stood out even brighter than it had that night when I was nearly ten. One of the warehouses had burned some years before, and the brick escarpment which walled the alley on the left was crumbling and broken with the black bones of charred timbers standing up against the night. The houses I passed were dead and boarded up; the shop fronts were broken, and the doors of three or four sagged open. But as I came to Number 52 it was as though nothing had changed. Nothing—in thirty years.

There was the same big window of heavy leaded panes so old and flawed that it was hard to see through them. There was the same mellow lamplight shining out into the street, and the same great door with its massive iron latch. And as I had thirty years before, I opened it and stepped into the shop.

The little bell tinkled as the door opened—a silver bell, it seemed, deep inside the shop. My footsteps rang on the scrubbed pine floor,

59

and the light of the three ship's lamps shone on the great tapestry that covered the right-hand wall, and on the counter and the cupboards to the left.

Under the center lamp, close beside the counter, was a little table of inlay and red enamel, and on it were a chessboard and men—ivory, black and red. I looked up from them, as I had thirty years before, and he stood there.

I think he knew me. I resemble my father, and it may have been that, but I think he knew me. As it happens I am not my father, and the game we played that night was a very different one.

"You are looking for something, sir?" It was the same soft voice, small and husky, trapped in his scarred throat. I had heard it often in my dreams during those thirty years. And he was the same, even to the clothes he wore. I could swear to it.

He repeated his question, and it was as though those thirty years had dissolved and it was a boy of nine-going-on-ten who stood half frightened, half defiant, and answered him: "I'd like to see a ship, I think. A ship in a bottle."

He might have been carved out of wood like one of his own fetishes. But his voice was not quite so soft and ingratiating as I remembered it. "I am sorry, sir. We have no ships."

I had changed the opening of the game, and the play was changing too. Very well; it was my move. "I'll look around, if you don't mind. I may see something that I like."

He took up the iron candlestick from the counter beside the little table. It looked smaller than I remembered, but then I had been smaller thirty years before. "Do you play chess, sir?" he inquired softly. "I have some very unusual men here—very old. Very fine. Will you look at them?"

There seemed to be a kind of pressure in the atmosphere, a web of intangible forces gathering around me, trying to push me back into the pattern of a generation before. I found myself standing over the table, holding one of the ivory men. So far as I could tell they were identical with those my father had won. I had them still at

60

home, all but one knight which had been lost.

"Thank you," I said. "I have a very fine set of my own—much like these of yours. They are Persian, I've been told."

I am not sure that he heard me. He stood holding the candlestick over his head, watching my face with those stony eyes. "I will play you for these men," he whispered.

"You must be confident," I said. "They are valuable."

He tried to smile, a quick grimace of that hard, thin mouth and a puckering of the scar across his jowl. "I trust my skill, sir," he replied. "Will you risk yours?"

I looked at him then, long and hard. That square brown face was no older than it had been thirty years before; the eyes were as bright

and hard and—ageless. I began to wonder then, as I think my father wondered suddenly as he rose the winner, what might be my forfeit if I should lose. But it was the defiant boy of ten who blurted out: "Yes—I'll play you. But not for these chessmen. I'll play you for a ship."

"There is no ship here," he repeated. "But if there is something else . . . ?"

"I'll see," I said. I turned to the counter and glanced over the hodgepodge of curios which littered it. They were less wonderful than they had seemed to a child who was not quite ten, trash mingled with fine workmanship and beautiful materials. I opened the door of a cupboard, and it seemed to me that the objects on the shelves were exactly as I had replaced them thirty years before. I pulled open a drawer, and the same colors and patterns of grotesque shells and gaudy butterflies came welling up in my memory.

I turned to him then and took the iron candlestick. It seemed to complete a kind of circuit in me—to drop a missing piece into the jigsaw that was shaping in my mind. Time melted away around me, and I was moving down the line of cupboards, opening one after another, touching the things in them quickly with my fingers as I held the candle high. This time the brown man was close beside me. And then I knew suddenly that this was it. I tugged at the cupboard door, and it stuck. I tugged again, and I thought that he had stopped breathing. And then something—chance, was it, or a kind of fate?—something gave me the trick, the little twist to the handle as I pulled, and the cupboard swung out on noiseless hinges exposing the alcove—and the ship.

It was the same—and it was not the same. The listless sails seemed browner and some of them were furled as though the captain had given up hope of wind. The deck was bleached whiter by the tropic sun, and the paint had chipped and blistered on the trim hull. The garments which the tiny crewmen wore were worn and shabby, and there were fewer men than I remembered. But the midget captain stood on his bridge as he had stood thirty years before, eyes fixed grimly on the empty sky, staring at me and through me. This time his hands were clasped behind his back, left fist clasped on his right wrist just above the shining hook. This time he seemed a little less erect, a little older than before.

I had a firm grip on the iron candlestick as I turned to the proprietor, for I did not like what was in his face. It was gone in an instant. "I had forgotten this, sir," he said. "I will play."

And then it seemed that there was another hand on mine, pushing my fingers down into the pocket of my vest, bringing out the same uneven little disc of gold which my father had tossed to call the play on another night.

His eyes went down to it, then back to mine. "If you are agreeable, sir," he said, "I am accustomed to the black."

I am not a great player, or even a very good one. As I set out the red men on the squares of the board, the same question rose again in the back of my mind. What was the price of my defeat? What was the prize he coveted, which I could give him—him, whose choice was always black?

I think that two of us played the white game that night. I think he knew it, for his seamed brown face was pale as he bent over the board. The game went quickly; there was never any doubt in my mind of the next move, and there seemed a grim certainty about his. I cannot tell you now what moves we made, or what the endplay was, but I knew suddenly that his king was trapped, and he knew too, for as I reached out to touch my queen his face was murderous.

Board and men went over on the floor as he lunged to his feet, but I was watching him and I sprang back over my toppled chair, sweeping up the heavy candlestick. As he lurched toward me, I hurled it at his head.

Was there a web of unseen forces spun around us, drawing us together after those thirty years? Was it chance, or fate? I could hardly have missed, but I did, and the iron stick crashed past him into the great green bubble with its imprisoned ship.

For one endless moment his iron fingers tore at my throat. For one moment I was beating blindly at his face with both fists, struggling to break away. For one moment he raged down at me, his face contorted with fear and rage, hissing strange syllables in that husky whisper. Then there welled up all around us the surge and roar of the sea, and I heard wind strumming through taut cordage, and the creak of straining blocks, and the snap of filling sails. I heard a great roaring voice shouting orders, and the answering cries of men. And something vast and black rushed past me through the gloom, the smell of the sea was rank in my nostrils, and the lights went out in a howl of rising wind—and the pressure of iron fingers on my throat was gone.

When I could breathe again I found my matches and lit the ship's lamp which hung from the beam overhead. The green glass globe was powder. The ship was gone. And the thing that lay sprawled at my feet among the scattered chessmen, its clothes in tatters and its flesh raked as if by the barnacles of a ship's bottom— its throat ripped as if by one slashing blow of a steel claw—that thing had been too long undersea to be wholly human.

*For hundreds of years she has sailed the stormy ocean, unable
to make port. But what brought this ship to her strange doom?*

The Flying Dutchman

AUGUSTE JAL

Many years ago there lived a ship's captain who went in fear of neither God nor all His saints. He was a Dutchman, it is said, but in what town he was born is not stated nor does it matter. He sailed all the seven seas in every weather imaginable. It was his boast that no storm, however terrible, could make him turn back.

On one voyage to the South, at the Cape of Good Hope, he ran into a head wind that might have blown the horns off an ox. Between the wind and the great waves the ship was in mortal danger. Everyone aboard argued with the captain to turn back.

"We are lost if you don't turn back, Captain!" they entreated him. "If you keep trying to round the Cape in this wind, we shall sink. We are all doomed, and there isn't even a priest on board to give us absolution before we die."

The Captain only laughed at the fears of his passengers and crew. Instead of heeding them he broke into songs so vile and blasphemous that just by themselves they might have drawn the lightning to strike the masts of the ship. Then he called for his pipe and his tankard of beer, and he smoked and drank as unconcernedly as though he were safe and snug in a tavern back home.

The others renewed their pleas to him to turn back, but the more they begged him the more obstinate he became. The wind snapped the masts, the sails were carried away, and he merely laughed and jeered at his terrified passengers.

Still more violently the storm raged, but the Captain treated with equal contempt the storm's violence and the fears of his crew and passengers. When his men tried to force him to turn and take shelter in a bay, he seized the ringleader in his arms and threw him overboard. As he did this, the clouds opened and a Shape alighted on the quarter deck of the ship. This Shape may have been the Almighty Himself, or was certainly sent by Him. Crew and passengers were struck dumb with terror. The Captain, however, went on smoking his pipe and did not even touch his cap as the Shape spoke to him.

"Captain," the Shape said, "you are a very obstinate man."

"And you," cried the Captain, "are a rascal! Who wants a smooth passage? Not I! I want nothing from you, so clear out and leave me unless you care to have your brains blown out."

The Shape shrugged his shoulder, without answering.

The Captain snatched up a pistol, cocked it and pulled the trigger. The bullet, however, instead of reaching its target turned and went through his hand. At that his rage knew no bounds. He leaped up to strike the Shape in the face. But even as he raised his arm it dropped limply at his side as though paralyzed. In helpless anger then he cursed and blasphemed, and called the heavenly Shape all kinds of evil names.

At this the Shape spoke to him.

"From this moment on, you are accursed. You are condemned

68

to sail forever without rest, without anchorage, without making
port of any kind. You shall never taste beer nor tobacco again.
Your drink will be gall; your meat will be red-hot iron. Only a
cabin boy will remain, of all your crew. Horns will grow from his
forehead and he will have a tiger's face and skin rougher than a
dogfish's."

At this the Captain, sobered at last, groaned. The Shape con-
tinued.

"It will always be your watch and you will never be able to
sleep, no matter how you long for it. The moment you close your
eyes a sword will pierce your body. And since you delight in tor-
menting sailors, you shall torment them forever more."

At that the Captain smiled. The Shape said to him:

"You shall be the evil spirit of the sea. You will travel all oceans and all latitudes without stopping or resting, and your ship will bring misfortune to all who sight it."

"Amen to that!" the Captain cried, and laughed.

"And on Judgment Day, Satan will claim you for his own."

"A fig for Satan!" the Captain answered.

The Shape vanished, and the Dutchman found himself alone with his cabin boy, who had already changed to the evil appearance that had been foretold. All the rest had vanished.

From that day to this the Flying Dutchman has sailed the seas, and he takes malicious pleasure in tricking unlucky mariners. He sets their ships on false courses, leads them onto uncharted shoals, and shipwrecks them. He turns their wine sour and changes all their food into beans. Sometimes he will pretend to be an ordinary ship and send letters on board other ships he meets at sea. If the other captain is so unfortunate as to try to read them, he is lost.

At other times an empty boat will draw alongside the Phantom Ship and vanish, a sure omen of bad luck to come. The Flying Dutchman can change the appearance of his ship at will, so that he cannot be recognized, and through the years he has collected around him a new crew. Every one of them comes from the worst criminals, pirates, and bullies of the world's oceans, and every one of them is as cursed and doomed as he himself.

*The monkey-faced visitor who always boarded the ship on
the second night out was a most unpleasant passenger indeed.*

Second Night Out

FRANK BELKNAP LONG

It was past midnight when I left my stateroom. The upper promenade deck was entirely deserted and thin wisps of fog hovered about the deck chairs and curled and uncurled about the gleaming rails. There was no air stirring. The ship moved forward sluggishly through a quiet, fog-enshrouded sea.

But I did not object to the fog. I leaned against the rail and inhaled the damp, murky air with a positive greediness. The almost unendurable nausea, the pervasive physical and mental misery had departed, leaving me serene and at peace. I was again capable of experiencing sensuous delight, and the aroma of the brine was not to be exchanged for pearls and rubies. I had paid in exorbitant coinage for what I was about to enjoy—for the five brief days of freedom and exploration in glamorous, sea-splendid Havana which

I had been promised by an enterprising and, I hoped, reasonably honest tourist agent. I am in all respects the antithesis of a wealthy man, and I had drawn so heavily upon my bank balance to satisfy the greedy demands of The Loriland Tours, Inc., that I had been compelled to renounce such really indispensable amenities as after-dinner cigars and ocean-privileged sherry and chartreuse.

But I was enormously content. I paced the deck and inhaled the moist, pungent air. For thirty hours I had been confined to my cabin with a sea illness more debilitating than bubonic plague or malignant sepsis, but having at length managed to squirm from beneath its iron heel I was free to enjoy my prospects. They were enviable and glorious. Five days in Cuba, with the privilege of driving up and down the sun-drenched Malecon in a flamboyantly upholstered limousine, and an opportunity to feast my discerning gaze on the pink walls of the Cabanas and the Columbus Cathedral and La Fuerza, the great storehouse of the Indies. Opportunity, also, to visit sunlit *patios,* and saunter by iron-barred *rejas,* and to sip *refrescos* by moonlight in open-air cafés, and to acquire, incidentally, a Spanish contempt for Big Business and the Strenuous Life. Then on to Haiti, dark and magical, and the Virgin Islands, and the quaint, incredible Old World harbor of Charlotte Amalie, with its chimneyless, red-roofed houses rising in tiers to the quiet stars; the natural Sargasso, the inevitable last port of call for rainbow fishes, diving boys and old ships with sun-bleached funnels and incurably drunken skippers. A flaming opal set in an amphitheater of malachite—its allure blazed forth through the gray fog and dispelled my northern spleen. I leaned against the rail and dreamed also of Martinique, which I would see in a few days. And then, suddenly, a dizziness came upon me. The ancient and terrible malady had returned to plague me.

Seasickness, unlike all other major afflictions, is a disease of the individual. No two people are ever afflicted with precisely the same symptoms. The manifestations range from a slight malaise to a devastating impairment of all one's faculties. I was afflicted with

74

the gravest symptoms imaginable. Choking and gasping, I left the rail and sank helplessly down into one of the three remaining deck chairs.

Why the steward had permitted the chairs to remain on deck was a mystery I couldn't fathom. He had obviously shirked a duty, for passengers did not habitually visit the promenade deck in the small hours, and foggy weather plays havoc with the wicker-work of steamer chairs. But I was too grateful for the benefits which his negligence had conferred upon me to be excessively critical. I lay sprawled at full length, grimacing and gasping and trying fervently to assure myself that I wasn't nearly as sick as I felt. And then, all at once, I became aware of an additional source of discomfiture.

The chair exuded an unwholesome odor. It was unmistakable. As I turned about, as my cheek came to rest against the damp varnished wood, my nostrils were assailed by an acrid and alien odor of a vehement, cloying potency. It was at once stimulating and indescribably repellent. In a measure, it assuaged my physical unease, but it also filled me with the most overpowering revulsion, with a sudden, hysterical and almost frenzied distaste.

I tried to rise from the chair, but the strength was gone from my limbs. An intangible presence seemed to rest upon me and weigh me down. And then the bottom seemed to drop out of everything. I am not being facetious. Something of the sort actually occurred. The *base* of the sane, familiar world vanished, was swallowed up. I sank down. Limitless gulfs seemed open beneath me, and I was immersed, lost in a gray void. The ship, however, did not vanish. The ship, the deck, the chair continued to support me, and yet, despite the retention of these outward symbols of reality, I was afloat in an unfathomable void. I had the illusion of falling, of sinking helplessly down through an eternity of space. It was as though the chair which supported me had passed into another dimension without ceasing to leave the familiar world—as though it floated simultaneously both in our three-dimensional world and in another world of alien, unknown dimensions. I became aware

of strange shapes and shadows all about me. I gazed through illim-
itable dark gulfs at continents and islands, lagoons, atolls, vast gray
waterspouts. I sank down into the great deep. I was immersed in
dark slime. The boundaries of sense were dissolved away, and the
breath of an active corruption blew through me, gnawing at my
vitals and filling me with extravagant torment. I was alone in the
great deep. And the shapes that accompanied me in my utter abys-
mal isolation were shriveled and black and dead, and they cavorted
deliriously with little monkey-heads with streaming, sea-drenched
viscera and putrid, pupilless eyes.

And then, slowly, the unclean vision dissolved. I was back again
in my chair and the fog was as dense as ever, and the ship moved
forward steadily through the quiet sea. But the odor was still pres-
ent—acrid, overpowering, revolting. I leapt from the chair, in pro-
found alarm. . . . I experienced a sense of having emerged from the
bowels of some stupendous and unearthly *encroachment,* of having
in a single instant exhausted the resources of earth's malignity, and
drawn upon untapped and intolerable reserves.

I got indoors somehow, into the warm and steamy interior of
the upper saloon, and waited, gasping, for the deck steward to come
to me. I had pressed a small button labeled "Deck Steward" in the
wainscoting adjoining the central stairway, and I frantically hoped
that he would arrive before it was too late, before the odor outside
percolated into the vast, deserted saloon.

The steward was a daytime official, and it was a cardinal crime
to fetch him from his berth at one in the morning. But I had to
have someone to talk to, and as the steward was responsible for the
chairs I naturally thought of him as the logical target for my inter-
rogations. He would *know.* He would be able to explain. The odor
would not be unfamiliar to him. He would be able to explain about
the chairs . . . about the chairs . . . about the chairs . . . I was grow-
ing hysterical and confused.

I wiped the perspiration from my forehead with the back of my
hand, and waited with relief for the steward to approach. He had

come suddenly into view above the top of the central stairway, and he seemed to advance toward me through a blue mist.

He was extremely solicitous, extremely courteous. He bent above me and laid his hand concernedly upon my arm. "Yes, sir. What can I do for you, sir? A bit under the weather, perhaps. What can I do?"

Do? Do? It was horribly confusing. I could only stammer: "The chairs, steward. On the deck. Three chairs. Why did you leave them there? Why didn't you take them inside?"

It wasn't what I had intended asking him. I had intended questioning him about the odor. But the strain, the shock, had confused me. The first thought that came into my mind on seeing the steward standing above me, so solicitous and concerned, was that he was a hypocrite and a scoundrel. He pretended to be concerned about me and yet out of sheer perversity he had prepared the snare which had reduced me to a pitiful and helpless wreck. He had left the chairs on deck deliberately, with a cruel and crafty malice, knowing all the time, no doubt, that *something* would occupy them.

But I wasn't prepared for the almost instant change in the man's demeanor. It was ghastly. Befuddled as I had become I could perceive at once that I had done him a grave, a terrible injustice. *He hadn't known.* All the blood drained out of his cheeks and his mouth fell open. He stood immobile before me, completely inarticulate, and for an instant I thought he was about to collapse, to sink helplessly down upon the floor.

"You saw—chairs?" he gasped at last.

I nodded.

The steward leaned toward me and gripped my arm. The flesh of his face was completely destitute of luster. From the parchment-white oval his two eyes, tumescent with fright, stared wildly down at me.

"It's the black, dead thing," he muttered. "The monkey-face. I *knew* it would come back. It always comes aboard at midnight on the second night out."

He gulped and his hand tightened on my arm.

"It's always on the second night out. It knows where I keep the chairs, and it takes them on deck and sits in them. I *saw* it last time. It was squirming about in the chair—lying stretched out and squirming horribly. Like an eel. It sits in all three of the chairs. When it saw me it got up and started toward me. But I got away. I came in here, and shut the door. But I saw it through the window."

The steward raised his arm and pointed.

"There. Through that window there. Its face was pressed against the glass. It was all black and shriveled and eaten away. A monkey-face, sir. So help me, the face of a dead, shriveled monkey. And wet—dripping. I was so frightened I couldn't breathe. I just stood and groaned, and then it went away."

He gulped.

"Doctor Blodgett was mangled, clawed to death at ten minutes to one. We heard his shrieks. The thing went back, I guess, and sat in the chairs for thirty or forty minutes after it left the window. Then it went down to Doctor Blodgett's stateroom and took his clothes. It was horrible. Doctor Blodgett's legs were missing, and his face was crushed to a pulp. There were claw marks all over him. And the curtains of his berth were drenched with blood.

"The captain told me not to talk. But I've got to tell someone. I can't help myself, sir. I'm afraid—I've got to talk. This is the third time it's come aboard. It didn't take anybody the first time, but it sat in the chairs. It left them all wet and slimy, sir—all covered with black, stinking slime."

I stared in bewilderment. What was the man trying to tell me? Was he completely unhinged? Or was I too confused, too ill myself to catch all that he was saying?

He went on wildly: "It's hard to explain, sir, but this boat is *visited*. Every voyage, sir—on the second night out. And each time it sits in the chairs. Do you understand?"

I didn't understand, clearly, but I murmured a feeble assent. My voice was appallingly tremulous and it seemed to come from the opposite side of the saloon.

"Something out there," I gasped. "It was awful. Out there, you hear? An awful odor. My brain. I can't imagine what's come over me, but I feel as though something were pressing on my brain. Here."

I raised my fingers and passed them across my forehead.

"Something here—something—"

The steward appeared to understand perfectly. He nodded and helped me to my feet. He was still self-engrossed, still horribly wrought up, but I could sense that he was also anxious to reassure and assist me.

"Stateroom 16D? Yes, of course. Steady, sir."

The steward had taken my arm and was guiding me toward the central stairway. I could hardly stand erect. My decrepitude was so apparent, in fact, that the steward was moved by compassion to the display of an almost heroic attentiveness. Twice I stumbled and would have fallen had not the guiding arm of my companion encircled my shoulders and levitated my sagging bulk.

"Just a few more steps, sir. That's it. Just take your time. There isn't anything will come of it, sir. You'll feel better when you're inside, with the fan going. Just take your time, sir."

At the door of my stateroom I spoke in a hoarse whisper to the man at my side. "I'm all right now. I'll ring if I need you. Just—let me—get inside. I want to lie down. Does this door lock from the inside?"

"Why, yes. Yes, of course. But maybe I'd better get you some water."

"No, don't bother. Just leave me—please."

"Well—all right, sir." Reluctantly the steward departed, after making certain that I had a firm grip on the handle of the door.

The stateroom was extremely dark. I was so weak that I was compelled to lean with all my weight against the door to close it. It shut with a slight click and the key fell out upon the floor. With a groan I went down on my knees and groveled apprehensively with my fingers on the soft carpet. But the key eluded me.

I cursed and was about to rise when my hand encountered something fibrous and hard. I started back, gasping. Then, frantically, my fingers slid over it, in a hectic effort at appraisal. It was—yes, undoubtedly a shoe. And sprouting from it, an ankle. The shoe reposed firmly on the floor of the stateroom. The flesh of the ankle, beneath the sock which covered it, was very cold.

In an instant I was on my feet, circling like a caged animal about the narrow dimensions of the stateroom. My hands slid over the walls, the ceiling. If only, dear God, the electric light button would not continue to elude me!

Eventually my hands encountered a rubbery excrescence on the smooth panels. I pressed, resolutely, and the darkness vanished to reveal a man sitting upright on a couch in the corner—a stout, well-dressed man holding a grip and looking perfectly composed. Only his face was invisible. His face was concealed by a handkerchief—a large handkerchief which had obviously been placed there intentionally, perhaps as a protection against the rather chilly air currents from the unshuttered port. The man was obviously asleep. He had not responded to the tugging of my hands on his ankles in the darkness, and even now he did not stir. The glare of the electric light bulbs above his head did not appear to annoy him in the least.

I experienced a sudden and overwhelming relief. I sat down beside the intruder and wiped the sweat from my forehead. I was still trembling in every limb, but the calm appearance of the man beside me was tremendously reassuring. A fellow passenger, no doubt, who had entered the wrong compartment. It should not be difficult to get rid of him. A mere tap on the shoulder, followed by a courteous explanation, and the intruder would vanish. A simple procedure, if only I could summon the strength to act with decision. I was so horribly enfeebled, so incredibly weak and ill. But at last I mustered sufficient energy to reach out my hand and tap the intruder on the shoulder.

"I'm sorry, sir," I murmured, "but you've got into the wrong stateroom. If I wasn't a bit under the weather I'd ask you to stay and smoke a cigar with me, but you see I"—with a distorted effort at a smile I tapped the stranger again nervously—"I'd rather be alone, so if you don't mind—sorry I had to wake you."

Immediately I perceived that I was being premature. I had not waked the stranger. The stranger did not budge, did not so much as agitate by his breathing the handkerchief which concealed his features.

I experienced a resurgence of my alarm. Tremulously I stretched forth my hand and seized a corner of the handkerchief. It was an

81

outrageous thing to do, but I had to know. If the intruder's face matched his body, if it was composed and familiar all would be well, but if for any reason—

The fragment of physiognomy revealed by the uplifted corner was not reassuring. With a gasp of affright I tore the handkerchief completely away. For a moment, a moment only, I stared at the dark and repulsive visage, with its staring, corpse-white eyes, viscid and malignant, its flat simian nose, hairy ears, and thick black tongue that seemed to leap up at me from out of the mouth. The face *moved* as I watched it, wriggled and squirmed revoltingly, while the head itself shifted its position, turning slightly to one side and revealing a profile more bestial and gangrenous and unclean than the brunt of his countenance.

I shrank back against the door, in frenzied dismay. I suffered as an animal suffers. My mind, deprived by shock of all capacity to form concepts, agonized instinctively, at a brutish level of consciousness. Yet through it all one mysterious part of myself remained horribly observant. I saw the tongue snap back into the mouth; saw the lines of the features shrivel and soften until presently from the slavering mouth and white sightless eyes there began to trickle thin streams of blood. In another moment the mouth was a red slit in a splotched horror of countenance—a red slit rapidly widening and dissolving in an amorphous crimson flood.

It took the steward nearly ten minutes to restore me. He was compelled to force spoonfuls of brandy between my tightly locked teeth, to bathe my forehead with ice water and to massage almost savagely my wrists and ankles. And when, finally, I opened my eyes he refused to meet them. He quite obviously wanted me to rest, to remain quiet, and he appeared to distrust his own emotional equipment. He was good enough, however, to enumerate the measures which had contributed to my restoration, and to enlighten me in respect to the *remnants:*

"The clothes were covered with blood, sir. I burned them."

On the following day he became more loquacious. "It was wearing the clothes of the gentleman who was killed last voyage, sir—it was wearing Doctor Blodgett's things. I recognized them instantly."

"But why—"

The steward shook his head. "I don't know, sir. Maybe your rushing up on deck saved you. Maybe it couldn't wait. It left a little after one the last time, sir, and it was later than that when I saw you to your stateroom. The ship may have passed out of its *zone,* sir. Or maybe it fell asleep and couldn't get back in time, and that's why it—dissolved. I don't think it's gone for good. There was blood on the curtains in Dr. Blodgett's cabin, and I'm afraid it always *goes* that way. It will come back next voyage, sir. I'm sure of it."

He cleared his throat.

"I'm glad you rang for me. If you'd gone right down to your stateroom it might be wearing your clothes next voyage."

Havana failed to restore me. Haiti was a black horror, a repellent quagmire of menacing shadows and alien desolation, and in Martinique I did not get a single hour of undisturbed sleep in my room at the hotel.

The Hemp

(A Virginia Legend from *Tiger Joy*)

STEPHEN VINCENT BENET

THE PLANTING OF THE HEMP

Captain Hawk scourged clean the seas
(Black is the gap below the plank)
From the Great North Bank to the Caribbees.
(Down by the marsh the hemp grows rank.)

His fear was on the seaport towns,
The weight of his hand held hard the downs.

And the merchants cursed him, bitter and black,
For a red flame in the sea-fog's wrack
Was all of their ships that might come back.

For all he had one word alone,
One clod of dirt in their faces thrown,
"The hemp that shall hang me is not grown!"

His name bestrode the seas like Death,
The waters trembled at his breath.

This is the tale of how he fell,
Of the long sweep and the heavy swell,
And the rope that dragged him down to hell.

The fight was done, and the gutted ship,
Stripped like a shark the sea-gulls strip,

84

Lurched blindly, eaten out with flame,
Back to the land from whence she came,
A skimming horror, an eyeless shame.

And Hawk stood up on his quarter-deck,
And saw the sky and saw the wreck.

Below, a butt for sailors' jeers,
White as the sky when a white squall nears,
Huddled the crowd of the prisoners.

Over the bridge of the tottering plank,
Where the sea shook and the gulf yawned blank,
They shrieked and struggled and dropped and sank.

Pinioned arms and hands bound fast.
One girl alone was left at last.

Sir Henry Gaunt was a mighty lord.
He sat in state at the Council board.

The governors were as naught to him
From one rim to the other rim.

Of his great plantations, flung out wide
Like a purple cloak, was a full month's ride.

Life and death in his white hands lay,
And his only daughter stood at bay,
Trapped like a hare in the toils that day.

He sat at wine in his gold and his lace,
And far away, in a bloody place,
Hawk came near, and she covered her face.

He rode in the fields, and the hunt was brave,
And far away, his daughter gave
A shriek that the seas cried out to hear,
And he could not see and he could not save.

.   .   .   .

THE GROWING OF THE HEMP

Sir Henry stood in the manor room,
And his eyes were hard gems in the gloom.

And he said, "Go, dig me furrows five
Where the green marsh creeps like a thing alive—
There at its edge where the rushes thrive."

And where the furrows rent the ground
He sowed the seed of hemp around.

.   .   .   .

And Hawk still scourges the Caribbees,
And many men kneel at his knees.

Sir Henry sits in his house alone,
And his eyes are hard and dull like stone.

And the waves beat, and the winds roar,
And all things are as they were before.

And the days pass, and the weeks pass,
And nothing changes but the grass.

86

Sir Henry's face is iron to mark,
And he gazes ever in the dark.

And the days pass, and the weeks pass,
And the world is as it always was.

But down by the marsh the sickles gleam,
Glitter on glitter, gleam on gleam,
And the hemp falls down by the stagnant stream.

And Hawk beats up from the Caribbees,
Swooping to pounce in the Northern seas.

Sir Henry sits sunk deep in his chair,
And white as his hand is grown his hair.

And the days pass, and the weeks pass,
And the sands roll from the hour-glass.

But down by the marsh, in the blazing sun,
The hemp is smoothed and twisted and spun.
The rope made, and the work done.

THE USING OF THE HEMP

Captain Hawk scourged clean the seas,
(Black is the gap below the plank)
From the Great North Bank to the Caribbees
(Down by the marsh the hemp grows rank)

He sailed in the broad Atlantic track
And the ships that saw him came not back.

Till once again, where the wide tides ran,
He stopped to harry a merchantman.

He bade her stop. Ten guns spake true
From her hidden ports, and a hidden crew,
Lacking his great ship through and through.

Dazed and dumb with the sudden death,
He scarce had time to draw a breath

Before the grappling-irons bit deep
And the boarders slew his crew like sheep.

88

Hawk stood up straight, his breast to the steel;
His cutlass made a bloody wheel.

His cutlass made a wheel of flame.
They shrank before him as he came.

And the bodies fell in a choking crowd,
And still he thundered out aloud,

"The hemp that shall hang me is not grown!"
They fled at last. He was left alone.

Before his foe Sir Henry stood.
"The hemp is grown and my word made good!"

And the cutlass clanged with a hissing whir
On the lashing blade of the rapier.

Hawk roared and charged like a maddened buck.
As the cobra strikes, Sir Henry struck,

Pouring his life in a single thrust,
And the cutlass shivered to sparks and dust.

Sir Henry stood on the blood-stained deck,
And set his foot on his foe's neck.

Then, from the hatch, where the torn decks slope,
Where the dead roll and the wounded grope,
He dragged the serpent of the rope.

The sky was blue and the sea was still,
The waves lapped softly, hill on hill,

And between one wave and another wave
The doomed man's cries were little and shrill.

The sea was blue and the sky was calm,
The air dripped with a golden balm.
Like a wind-blown fruit between sea and sun,
A black thing writhed at a yard-arm.

Slowly then, and awesomely,
The ship sank, and the gallows-tree,
And there was nought between sea and sun—
Nought but the sun and the sky and the sea.

But down by the marsh, where the fever breeds,
Only the water chuckles and pleads;
For the hemp clings fast to a dead man's throat,
And blind Fate gathers back her seeds.

The ship came from the bottom of the ocean, and the cargo she carried was one of treasure and horror.

The Stone Ship

WILLIAM HOPE HODGSON

Rum things! Of course there are rum things happen at sea—as rum as ever there were. I remember when I was in the *Alfred Jessop,* a small barque whose owner was her skipper, we came across a most extraordinary thing.

We were twenty days out from London, and well down into the tropics. I was in the fo'cas'le. The day had passed without a breath of wind, and the night found us with all the lower sails up in the buntlines.

Now, I want you to take good note of what I am going to say:

When it was dark in the second dog watch, there was not a sail in sight; not even the far-off smoke of a steamer, and no land nearer than Africa, about a thousand miles to the eastward of us.

It was our watch on deck from eight to twelve, midnight, and my lookout from eight to ten. For the first hour, I walked to and fro across the break of the fo'cas'le head, smoking my pipe and just listening to the quiet. . . . Ever heard the kind of silence you can get away out at sea? You need to be in one of the old-time windjammers, with all the lights dowsed, and the sea as calm and quiet as some queer plain of death. And then you want a pipe and the lonesomeness of the fo'cas'le head, with the caps'n to lean against while you listen and think. And all about you, stretching out into the miles, only and always the enormous silence of the sea, spreading out a thousand miles every way into the everlasting, brooding night. And not a light anywhere, out on all the waste of waters; nor ever a sound, as I have told, except the faint moaning of the masts and gear, as they chafe and whine a little to the occasional invisible roll of the ship.

And suddenly, across all this silence, I heard Jensen's voice from the head of the starboard steps say:

"Did you hear *that,* Duprey?"

"What?" I asked, cocking my head up. But as I questioned, I heard what he heard—the constant sound of running water, for all the world like the noise of a brook running down a hillside. And the queer sound was surely not a hundred fathoms off our port bow!

"By gum!" said Jensen's voice, out of the darkness. "That's funny!"

"Shut up!" I whispered, and went across, in my bare feet, to the port rail, where I leaned out into the darkness, and stared towards the curious sound.

The noise of a brook running down a hillside continued, where there was no brook for a thousand sea miles in any direction.

"What is it?" said Jensen's voice again, scarcely above a whisper now. From below him on the main deck there came several voices questioning: "Hark!" "Stow the talk!" ". . . there!" "Listen!" "Lord love us, what is it?" . . . And then Jensen muttering to them to be quiet.

There followed a full minute during which we all heard the

brook, where no brook could ever run; and then, out of the night there came a sudden hoarse incredible sound: OOAAZE, OOOAZE, ARRRR, ARRRR, OOOAZE—a stupendous sort of croak, deep and somehow abominable, out of the blackness. In the same instant, I found myself sniffing the air. There was a queer rank smell stealing through the night.

"Forrard there on the lookout!" I heard the mate singing out, away aft. "Forrard there! What the blazes are you doing!"

I heard him come clattering down the port ladder from the poop, and then the sound of his feet at a run along the main deck. Simultaneously, there was a thudding of bare feet as the watch below came racing out of the fo'cas'le beneath me.

"Now then! Now then! Now then!" shouted the mate, as he charged up on the fo'cas'le head. "What's up?"

"It's something off the port bow, sir," I said. "Running water! And then that sort of howl. . . . Your night glasses," I suggested.

"Can't see a thing," he growled, as he stared away through the dark. "There's a sort of mist. Phoo! What a devil of a stink!"

"Look!" said someone down on the main deck. "What's that?"

I saw it in the same instant, and caught the mate's elbow.

"Look, sir," I said. "There's a light there, about three points off the bow. It's moving."

The mate was staring through his night glasses, and suddenly he thrust them into my hands.

"See if you can make it out," he said, and forthwith put his hands around his mouth, and bellowed into the night: "Ahoy there! Ahoy there! Ahoy there!" his voice going out lost into the silence and darkness all around. But there came never a comprehensible answer, only all the time the infernal noise of a brook running out there on the sea, a thousand miles from any brook of earth; and away on the port bow, a vague shapeless shining.

I put the glasses to my eyes, and stared. The light was bigger and brighter, seen through the binoculars; but I could make nothing of it, only a dull, elongated shining that moved vaguely in the darkness, apparently a hundred fathoms or so away on the sea.

"Ahoy there! Ahoy there!" sang out the mate again. Then, to the man below: "Quiet there on the main deck!"

There followed about a minute of intense stillness, during which we all listened; but there was no sound, except the constant noise of water running steadily.

I was watching the curious shining, and I saw it flick out suddenly at the mate's shout. Then in a moment I saw three dull lights, one under the other, that flicked in and out intermittently.

"Here, give me the glasses!" said the mate, and grabbed them from me.

He stared intensely for a moment; then he swore, and turned to me.

"What do you make of them?" he asked abruptly.

"I don't know, sir," I said. "I'm just puzzled. Perhaps it's electricity, or something of that sort."

"Lord!" he said for the second time. "What a stink!"

As he spoke, there came a most extraordinary thing; for there sounded a series of heavy reports out of the darkness, seeming, in the silence, almost as loud as the sound of small cannon.

"They're shooting!" shouted a man on the main deck, suddenly.

The mate said nothing; only he sniffed violently at the night air. "By gum!" he muttered. "What is it?"

I put my hand over my nose; for there was a terrible, charnel-like stench filling all the night about us.

"Take my glasses, Duprey," said the mate, after a few minutes of further watching. "Keep an eye over yonder. I'm going to call the Captain."

He pushed his way down the ladder, and hurried aft. About five minutes later, he returned forrard with the Captain and the second and third mates, all in their shirts and trousers.

"Anything fresh, Duprey?" asked the mate.

"No, sir," I said, and handed him back his glasses. "The lights have gone again, and I think the mist is thicker. There's still the sound of running water out there."

The Captain and the three mates stood some time along the port rail of the fo'cas'le head, watching through their night glasses, and listening. Twice the mate hailed, but there came no reply.

There was some talk among the officers, and I gathered that the Captain was thinking of investigating.

"Clear one of the lifeboats, Mr. Gelt," he said at last. "The glass is steady; there'll be no wind for hours yet. Pick out half a dozen men. Take 'em out of either watch, if they want to come. I'll be back when I've got my coat."

"Away aft with you, Duprey, and some of you others," said the mate. "Get the cover off the port lifeboat, and bail her out."

"Aye, aye, sir," I answered, and went away aft with the others.

We had the boat into the water within twenty minutes, which is good time for a windjammer.

I was one of the men told off to the boat, with two others from our watch, and one from the starboard.

The Captain came down the end of the main tops'l halyards into the boat, and the third mate after him. The third mate took the tiller, and gave orders to cast off.

We pulled out clear of our vessel, and the Skipper told us to lie on our oars for a moment while he took his bearings. He leaned forward to listen, and we all did the same. The sound of the running water was quite distinct across the quietness, but it struck me as seeming not so loud as earlier.

I remember now that I noticed how plain the mist had become— a sort of warm, wet mist; not a bit thick, but just enough to make the night very dark, and to be visible, eddying slowly in a thin vapor around the port side-light, looking like a red cloudiness swirling lazily through the red glow of the big lamp.

There was no other sound at this time beyond the sound of the running water; and the Captain, after handing something to the third mate, gave the order to give way.

I was rowing stroke, and close to the officers, and so was able to see dimly that the Captain had passed a heavy revolver over to the third mate.

"Ho!" I thought to myself. "So the Old Man's a notion there's really something dangerous over there."

I slipped a hand quickly behind me, and felt that my sheath knife was clear.

We pulled easily for about three or four minutes, with the sound of the water growing plainer somewhere ahead in the darkness. Astern of us, a vague red glowing through the night and vapor showed where our vessel was lying.

We were rowing easily, when suddenly the bow oar muttered, "G'lord!" Immediately afterwards, there was a loud splashing in the water on his side of the boat.

"What's wrong in the bows there?" asked the Skipper sharply.

"There's somethin' in the water, sir, messing round my oar," said the man.

I stopped rowing, and looked around. All the men did the same. There was a further sound of splashing, and the water was driven right over the boat in showers. Then the bow oar called out: "There's somethin' got a holt of my oar, sir!"

I could tell the man was frightened; and I knew suddenly that a curious nervousness had come to me—a vague, uncomfortable dread, such as the memory of an ugly tale will bring in a lonesome place. I believe every man in the boat had a similar feeling. It seemed to me in that moment that a definite, muggy sort of silence was all around us, and this in spite of the sound of the splashing, and the strange noise of the running water somewhere ahead of us on the dark sea.

"It's let go the oar, sir!" said the man.

Abruptly, as he spoke, there came the Captain's voice in a roar: "Back water all!" he shouted. "Put some beef into it now! Back all! Back all! . . . Why the devil was no lantern put in the boat! Back now! Back! Back!"

We backed fiercely, with a will; for it was plain that the Old Man had some good reason to get the boat away pretty quickly. He was right, too; though whether it was guesswork or some kind of instinct that made him shout out at that moment, I don't know; only I am sure he could not have seen anything in that absolute darkness.

As I was saying, he was right in shouting to us to back; for we had not backed more than half a dozen fathoms when there was a tremendous splash right ahead of us, as if a house had fallen into the sea; and a regular wave of sea water came at us out of the darkness, throwing our bows up, and soaking us fore and aft.

"Good Lord!" I heard the third mate gasp out. "What's that?"

"Back all! Back! Back!" the Captain sang out again.

After some moments, he had the tiller put over, and told us to pull. We gave way with a will, as you may think, and in a few minutes were alongside our own ship again.

"Now then, men," the Captain said, when we were safe aboard, "I'll not order any of you to come; but after the steward's served out a tot of grog each, those who are willing can come with me, and we'll have another go at finding out what devil's work is going on over yonder."

He turned to the mate, who had been asking questions:

"Say, Mister," he said, "it's no sort of thing to let the boat go without a lamp aboard. Send a couple of the lads into the lamp locker, and pass out a couple of the anchor lights and that deck bull's-eye you use at nights for clearing up the ropes."

He whipped round on the third mate: "Tell the steward to buck up with that grog, Mr. Andrews," he said, "and while you're there, pass out the axes from the rack in my cabin."

The grog came along a minute later, and then the third mate with three big axes from the cabin rack.

"Now then, men," said the Skipper, "those who are coming with me had better take an ax each from the third mate. They're mighty good weapons in any sort of trouble."

We all stepped forward, and he burst out laughing, slapping his thigh.

"That's the kind of thing I like!" he said. "Mr. Andrews, the axes won't go round. Pass out that old cutlass from the steward's pantry. It's a pretty hefty piece of iron!"

The old cutlass was brought, and the man who was short of an ax collared it. By this time, two of the 'prentices had filled (at least we supposed they had filled them!) two of the ship's anchor lights; also they had brought out the bull's-eye lamp we used when clearing up the ropes on a dark night. With the lights and the axes and the cutlass, we felt ready to face anything, and down we went again into the boat, with the Captain and the third mate after us.

"Lash one of the lamps to one of the boat hooks, and rig it out over the bows," ordered the Captain.

This was done, and in this way the light lit up the water for a couple of fathoms ahead of the boat and made us feel less that something could come at us without our knowing. Then the painter was cast off, and we gave way again toward the sound of the running water out there in the darkness.

I remember now that it struck me that our vessel had drifted a bit, for the sounds seemed farther away. The second anchor light had been put in the stern of the boat, and the third mate kept it between his feet while he steered. The Captain had the bull's-eye in his hand, and was pricking up the wick with his pocketknife.

As we pulled, I took a glance or two over my shoulder but could see nothing, except the lamp making a yellow halo in the mist around the boat's bows as we forged ahead. Astern of us, on our quarter, I could see the dull red glow of our vessel's port light. That was all, and not a sound in all the sea, as you might say, except the roll of our oars in the rowlocks, and somewhere in the darkness ahead, that curious noise of water running steadily; now sounding, as I have said, fainter and seeming farther away.

"It's got my oar again, sir!" exclaimed the man at the bow oar suddenly, and he jumped to his feet. He hove his oar up with a great splashing of water into the air, and immediately something whirled and beat about in the yellow halo of light over the bows of the boat. There was a crash of breaking wood, and the boat hook was broken. The lamp soused down into the sea, and was lost. Then in the darkness there was a heavy splash, and a shout from the bow oar: "It's loosed off the oar!"

"Vast pulling, all!" sang out the Skipper. Not that the order was necessary, for not a man was pulling. The Skipper had jumped up, and whipped a big revolver out of his coat pocket.

He had this in his right hand, and the bull's-eye in his left. He stepped forrard smartly over the oars from thwart to thwart, till he reached the bows, where he shone his light down into the water.

"My word!" he said. "Lord in Heaven! Saw anyone ever the like!"

And I doubt whether any man ever did see what we saw then; for the water was thick and living for yards around the boat with the hugest eels I ever saw before or after.

"Give way, men," said the Skipper, after a minute. "Yon's no explanation of the almighty queer sounds out yonder we're hearing this night. Give way, lads!"

He stood right up in the bows of the boat, shining his bull's-eye from side to side, and flashing it down on the water.

"Give way, lads!" he said again. "They don't like the light; that'll keep them from the oars. Give way steady now. Mr. Andrews, keep her dead on for the noise out yonder."

We pulled for some minutes, during which I felt my oar plucked at twice; but a flash of the Captain's lamp seemed sufficient to make the brutes loose hold.

The noise of the water running appeared now quite near-sounding. About this time, I had a sense again of an added sort of silence to all the natural quietness of the sea. And I had a return of the curious nervousness that had touched me before. I kept listening intensely, as if I expected to hear some sound other than the noise of the water. It came to me suddenly that I had the kind of feeling one has in the aisle of a large cathedral. There was a sort of echo in the night—an incredibly faint reduplicating of the noise of our oars.

"Hark!" I said audibly, not realizing at first that I was speaking aloud. "There's an echo ——"

"That's it!" the Captain cut in sharply. "I thought I heard something rummy!"

. . . "I thought I heard something rummy," said a thin ghostly echo out of the night. ". . . thought I heard something rummy. . . . heard something rummy." The words went muttering and whispering to and fro in the night about us in rather a horrible fashion.

"Good Lord!" said the Old Man in a whisper.

We had all stopped rowing, and were staring about us into the thin mist that filled the night. The Skipper was standing with the bull's-eye lamp held over his head, circling the beam of light around from port to starboard and back again.

Abruptly, as he did so, it came to me that the mist was thinner. The sound of the running water was very near, but it gave back no echo.

"The water doesn't echo, sir," I said. "That's funny!"

"That's funny," came back at me, from the darkness to port and starboard, in a multitudinous muttering. . . . "Funny! . . . funny . . . eeey!"

"Give way!" said the Old Man loudly. "I'll bottom this!"

"I'll bottom this. . . . Bottom this . . . this!" The echo came back in a veritable rolling of unexpected sound. And then we dipped our oars again, and the night was full of the reiterated rolling echoes of our rowlocks.

Suddenly the echoes ceased and there was, strangely, the sense of a great space about us. In the same moment the sound of the water running appeared to be directly before us, but somehow up in the air.

"Vast rowing!" said the Captain, and we lay on our oars, staring around into the darkness ahead. The Old Man swung the beam of his lamp upwards, making circles with it in the night, and abruptly I saw something looming vaguely through the thinner-seeming mist.

"Look, sir," I called to the Captain. "Quick, sir, your light right above you! There's something up there!"

The Old Man flashed his lamp upwards, and found the thing I had seen. But it was too indistinct to make anything of, and even as he saw it, the darkness and mist seemed to wrap it about.

"Pull a couple of strokes, all!" said the Captain. "Stow your talk, there in the boat! . . . Again! . . . . That'll do! Vast pulling!"

He was sending the beam of his lamp constantly across that part of the night where we had seen the thing, and suddenly I saw it again.

"There, sir!" I said. "A little to starboard with the light."

He flicked the light swiftly to the right, and immediately we all saw the thing plainly—a strangely-made mast standing up there out of the mist, and looking like no spar I had ever seen.

It seemed now that the mist must lie pretty low on the sea in places, for the mast stood up out of it plainly for several fathoms; but, lower, it was hidden in the mist which, I thought, seemed heavier now all around us; but thinner, as I have said, above.

"Ship ahoy!" sang out the Skipper suddenly. "Ship ahoy, there!" But for some moments there came never a sound back to us except the constant noise of the water running not a score of yards away; and then, it seemed to me that a vague echo beat back at us out of the mist, oddly: "Ahoy! Ahoy! Ahoy!"

"There's something hailing us, sir," said the third mate.

Now, that "something" was significant. It showed the sort of feeling that was on us all.

"That's na ship's mast as ever I've seen!" I heard the man next to me mutter. "It's got a unnatcheral look."

"Ahoy there!" shouted the Skipper again, at the top of his voice. "Ahoy there!"

With the suddenness of a clap of thunder there burst out at us a vast grunting: OOOAZE; ARRRR; ARRRR; OOOAZE—a volume of sound so great that it seemed to make the loom of the oar in my hand vibrate.

"Good Lord!" said the Captain, and leveled his revolver into the mist; but he did not fire.

I had loosed one hand from my oar, and gripped my ax. I remember thinking that the Skipper's pistol wouldn't be of much use against whatever thing made a noise like that.

"It wasn't ahead, sir," said the third mate abruptly, from where he sat and steered. "I think it came from somewhere over to starboard."

"What a devil of a stink!" said the Skipper. "Pass that other anchor light forrard."

I reached for the lamp, and handed it to the next man, who passed it on.

"The other boat hook," said the Skipper; and when he'd got it, he lashed the lamp to the hook end, and then lashed the whole arrangement upright in the bows, so that the lamp was well above his head.

"Now," he said. "Give way gently! And stand by to back water if I tell you. . . . Watch my hand, Mister," he added to the third mate. "Steer as I tell you."

We rowed a dozen slow strokes, and with every stroke I took a look over my shoulder. The Captain was leaning forward under the big lamp, with the bull's-eye in one hand and his revolver in the other. He kept flashing the beam of the lantern up into the night.

"Good Lord!" he said, suddenly. "Vast pulling."

We stopped, and I slewed around on the thwart and stared.

The Captain was standing under the glow of the anchor light, and shining the bull's-eye up at a great mass that loomed dully through the mist. As he flicked the light to and fro over the great bulk, I realized that the boat was within some three or four fathoms of the hull of a vessel.

"Pull another stroke," the Skipper said in a quiet voice, after a few minutes of silence. "Gently now! Gently! . . . Vast pulling!"

I slewed around again on my thwart and stared. I could see part of the thing quite distinctly now, and more of it as I followed the beam of the Captain's lantern. She was a vessel right enough, but such a vessel as I had never seen. She was extraordinarily high out of the water, seemed very short, and rose up into a queer mass at one end. But what puzzled me more than anything else, I think, was the queer look of her sides, down which water was streaming all the time.

"That explains the sound of the water running," I thought to myself. "But what on earth is she built of?"

You will understand a little of my bewildered feelings when I tell you that, as the beam of the Captain's lamp shone on the side of this queer vessel, it showed stone everywhere—as if she were built out of stone. I never felt so dumbfounded in my life.

"She's stone, Cap'n!" I said. "Look at her, sir!"

I realized, as I spoke, a certain horribleness, of the unnatural. . . . A stone ship, floating out there in the night in the midst of the lonely Atlantic.

"She's stone," I said again, in that absurd way in which one reiterates when one is bewildered.

"Look at the slime on her!" muttered the man next but one forrard of me. "She's a proper Davy Jones ship. By gum! She stinks like a corpse!"

"Ship ahoy!" roared the Skipper at the top of his voice. "Ship ahoy! Ship ahoy!"

His shout beat back at us in a curious, dank, yet metallic echo, something the way one's voice sounds in an old disused quarry.

"There's no one aboard there, sir," said the third mate. "Shall I put the boat alongside?"

"Yes, shove her up, Mister," said the Old Man. "I'll bottom this business. Pull a couple of strokes, aft there! In bow, and stand by to fend off."

The third mate laid the boat alongside, and we unshipped our oars.

Then I leaned forward over the side of the boat, and pressed the flat of my hand upon the stark side of the ship. The water that ran down her side sprayed out over my hand and wrist in a cataract;

105

but I did not think about being wet, for my hand was pressed solid upon stone. . . . I pulled my hand back with a queer feeling.

"She's stone, right enough, sir," I said to the Captain.

"We'll soon see what she is," he said. "Shove your oar up against her side, and shin up. We'll pass the lamp up to you as soon as you're aboard. Shove your ax in the back of your belt. I'll cover you with my gun till you're aboard."

"Aye, aye, sir," I said, though I felt a bit funny at the thought of having to be the first aboard that rummy craft.

I put my oar upright against her side, and took a spring up it from the thwart. In a moment I was grabbing over my head for her rail, with every rag on me soaked through with the water that was streaming down her and spraying out over the oar and me.

I got a firm grip of the rail, and hoisted my head high enough to look over; but I could see nothing . . . what with the darkness, and the water in my eyes.

I knew it was no time for going slow, if there were danger aboard; so I went in over that rail in one spring, my boots coming down with a horrible, ringing, hollow, stony sound on her decks. I whipped the water out of my eyes and the ax out of my belt all in the same moment. Then I took a good stare fore and aft; but it was too dark to see anything.

"Come along, Duprey!" shouted the Skipper. "Collar the lamp."

I leaned out sideways over the rail, and grabbed for the lamp with my left hand, keeping the ax ready in my right and staring inboard; for I tell you, I was just mortally afraid in that moment of what might be aboard her.

I felt the lamp ring with my left hand, and gripped it. Then I switched it aboard, and turned fair and square to see where I'd gotten.

Now, you never saw such a packet as that, not in a hundred years, nor yet two hundred, I should think. She'd got a rum little main deck about forty feet long, and then came a step about two feet high, and another bit of a deck, with a little house on it.

That was the after end of her; and more I couldn't see, because the light of my lamp went no farther, except to show me vaguely the big, cocked-up stern of her going up into the darkness. I never saw a vessel made like her; not even in an old picture of old-time ships.

Forrard of me was her mast—a big lump of a stick it was, too, for her size. And here was another amazing thing: the mast of her looked to be just solid stone.

"Funny, isn't she, Duprey?" said the Skipper's voice at my back, and I came round on him with a jump.

"Yes," I said. "I'm puzzled. Aren't you, sir?"

"Well," he said, "I am. If we were like the shellbacks they talk of in books, we'd be crossing ourselves. But, personally, give me a good heavy Colt, or the hefty chunk of steel you're cuddling."

He turned from me, and put his head over the rail.

"Pass up the painter, Jales," he said, to the bow oar. Then to the third mate:

"Bring 'em all up, Mister. If there's going to be anything rummy, we may as well make a picnic party of the lot. . . . Hitch that painter round the cleet yonder, Duprey," he added to me. "It looks good solid stone! . . . That's right. Come along."

He swung the thin beam of his lantern fore and aft, and then forrard again.

"Lord!" he said. "Look at that mast. It's stone. Give it a whack with the back of your ax, man; only remember she's apparently a bit of an oldtimer! So go gently."

I took my ax short, and tapped the mast, and it rang dull, and solid, like a stone pillar. I struck it again, harder, and a sharp flake of stone flew past my cheek. The Skipper thrust his lantern close up to where I'd struck the mast.

"By George," he said, "she's absolute a stone ship—solid stone, afloat here out of Eternity, in the middle of the wide Atlantic. . . . Why! She must weigh a thousand tons more than she's buoyancy to carry. It's just impossible. . . . It's ——"

He turned his head quickly at a sound in the darkness along the decks. He flashed his light that way, across and across the after decks; but we could see nothing.

"Get a move on you in the boat!" he said sharply, stepping to the rail and looking down. "For once I'd really prefer a little more of your company. . . ." He came around like a flash. "Duprey, what was that?" he asked in a low voice.

"I certainly heard something, sir," I said. "I wish the others would hurry. By jove! Look! What's that?"

"Where?" he said, and sent the beam of his lamp to where I pointed with my ax.

"There's nothing," he said, after circling the light all over the deck. "Don't go imagining things. There's enough solid unnatural fact here without trying to add to it."

There came the splash and thud of feet behind, as the first of the men came up over the side and jumped clumsily into the lee scuppers, which had water in them. You see she had a cant to that side, and I suppose the water had collected there.

The rest of the men followed, and then the third mate. That made six of us, all well armed; and I felt a bit more comfortable, as you can think.

"Hold up that lamp of yours, Duprey, and lead the way," said the Skipper. "You're getting the post of honor this trip!"

"Aye, aye, sir," I said, and stepped forward, holding up the lamp in my left hand, and carrying my ax halfway down the haft, in my right.

"We'll try aft, first," said the Captain, and led the way himself, flashing the bull's-eye to and fro. At the raised portion of the deck, he stopped.

"Now," he said in his queer way, "let's have a look at this. . . . Tap it with your ax, Duprey. . . . Ah!" he added, as I hit it with the back of my ax. "That's what we call stone at home, right enough. She's just as rum as anything I've seen while I've been fishing. We'll go on aft and have a peep into the deckhouse. Keep your axes

108

handy, men."

We walked slowly up to the curious little house, the deck rising to it with quite a slope. At the foreside of the little deckhouse, the Captain pulled up, and shone his bull's-eye down at the deck. I saw that he was looking at what was plainly the stump of the after mast. He stepped closer to it, and kicked it with his foot; and it gave out the same dull, solid note that the foremast had done. It was obviously a chunk of stone.

I held up my lamp so that I could see the upper part of the house more clearly. The fore-part had two square window spaces in it, but there was no glass in either of them; and the blank darkness within the queer little place just seemed to stare out at us.

And then I saw something suddenly . . . a great shaggy head of red hair was rising slowly into sight, through the port window, the one nearest to us.

"My God! What's that, Cap'n?" I called out. But it was gone, even as I spoke.

"What?" he asked, jumping at the way I had sung out.

"At the port window, sir," I said. "A great red-haired head. It came right up to the window place, and then it went in a moment."

The Skipper stepped right up to the little dark window, and pushed his lantern through into the blackness. He flashed a light around, then withdrew the lantern.

"Bosh, man!" he said. "That's twice you've got fancying things. Ease up your nerves a bit!"

"I did see it!" I said, almost angrily. "It was like a great red-haired head. . . ."

"Stow it, Duprey!" he said, though not sneeringly. "The house is absolutely empty. Come round to the door, if the Infernal Masons that built her went in for doors! Then you'll see for yourself. All the same, keep your axes ready, lads. I've a notion there's something pretty queer aboard here."

We went up around the after-end of the little house, and here we saw what appeared to be a door.

The Skipper felt at the queer, odd-shapen handle, and pushed at the door; but it had stuck fast.

"Here, one of you!" he said, stepping back. "Have a whack at this with your ax. Better use the back."

One of the men stepped forward, and we stood away to give him room. As his ax struck, the door went to pieces with exactly the same sound that a thin slab of stone would make when broken.

"Stone!" I heard the Captain mutter under his breath. "By gum! What is she?"

I did not wait for the Skipper. He had put me a bit on edge, and I stepped bang in through the open doorway, with the lamp high, and holding my ax short and ready; but there was nothing in the place save a stone seat running all around, except where the doorway opened on to the deck.

"Find your red-haired monster?" asked the Skipper, at my elbow.

I said nothing. I was suddenly aware that he was all on the jump with some inexplicable fear. I saw his glance going everywhere about him. And then his eye caught mine, and he saw that I realized. He was a man almost callous to fear; that is, the fear of danger in what I might call any normal seafaring shape. And this palpable nerviness affected me tremendously. He was obviously doing his best to throttle it, and trying all he knew to hide it. I had a sudden warmth of understanding for him, and dreaded lest the men should realize his state. Funny that I should be able at that moment to be aware of anything but my own bewildered fear and expectancy of intruding upon something monstrous at any instant. Yet I describe exactly my feelings as I stood there in the house.

"Shall we try below, sir?" I said, and turned to where a flight of stone steps led down into an utter blackness, out of which rose a strange, dank scent of the sea . . . an imponderable mixture of brine and darkness.

"The worthy Duprey leads the van!" said the Skipper; but I felt no irritation now. I knew that he must cover his fright until he had got control again; and I think he felt, somehow, that I was backing him up. I remember now that I went down those stairs into that unknowable and ancient cabin, as much aware in that moment of the Captain's state as of that extraordinary thing I had just seen at the little window, or of my own half-funk of what we might see any moment.

The Captain was at my shoulder as I went, and behind him came the third mate, and then the men, all in single file; for the stairs were narrow.

I counted seven steps down, and then my foot splashed into water on the eighth. I held the lamp low and stared. I had caught no glimpse of a reflection, and I saw now that this was owing to a curious, dull, grayish scum that lay thinly on the water, seeming to match the color of the stone which composed the steps and bulkheads.

"Stop!" I said. "I'm in water!"

I let my foot down slowly, got the next step, then sounded with my ax, and found the floor at the bottom. I stepped down and stood up to my thighs in water.

"It's all right, sir," I said, suddenly whispering. I held my lamp up, and glanced quickly about me.

"It's not deep. There's two doors here. . . ."

I whirled my ax up as I spoke; for suddenly I had realized that one of the doors was open a little. It seemed to move, as I stared, and I could have imagined that a vague undulation ran towards me, across the dull scum-covered water.

"The door's opening!" I said aloud, with a sudden sick feeling. "Look out!"

I backed from the door, staring; but nothing came. And abruptly, I had control of myself; for I realized that the door was not moving. It had not moved at all. It was simply ajar.

"It's all right, sir," I said. "It's not opening."

I stepped forward again a pace towards the doors, as the Skipper and the third mate came down with a jump, splashing the water all over me.

The Captain still had the "nerves" on him, as I think I could feel even then; but he hid it well.

"Try the door, Mister. I've jumped my lamp out!" he growled to the third mate, who pushed at the door on my right; but it would not open beyond the nine or ten inches it was fixed ajar.

"There's this one here, sir," I whispered, and held my lantern up to the closed door that lay on my left.

"Try it," said the Skipper, in an undertone. We did so, but it also was fixed. I whirled my ax suddenly, and struck the door heavily in the center of the main panel. The whole thing crashed into flinders of stone that went with hollow-sounding splashes into the darkness beyond.

"Goodness!" said the Skipper in a startled voice, for my action had been so instant and unexpected. He covered his lapse in a moment by the warning:

"Look out for bad air!" But I was already inside with the lamp, and holding my ax handily. There was no bad air; for right across from me was a split, clean through the ship's side, that I could have put my two arms through, just above the level of the scummy water.

The place I had broken into was a cabin of a kind; but it seemed strange and dank, and too narrow to breathe in; and wherever I turned, I saw stone. The third mate and the Skipper gave simultaneous expressions of disgust at the wet dismalness of the place.

"It's all stone," I said, and brought my ax hard against the front of a sort of squat cabinet, which was built into the after bulkhead. It caved in, with a crash of splintered stone.

"Empty!" I said, and turned instantly away.

The Skipper and the third mate, with the men who were now peering in at the door, crowded out; and in that moment, I pushed my ax under my arm, and thrust my hand into the burst stone chest. Twice I did this, with almost the speed of lightning, and shoved what I had seen into the side pocket of my coat. Then I was following the others; and not one of them had noticed a thing. As for me, I was quivering with excitement, so that my knees shook;

for I had caught the unmistakable gleam of gems, and had grabbed for them in that one swift instant.

I wonder whether anyone can realize what I felt in that moment. I knew that, if my guess were right, I had snatched the power, in that one miraculous moment, that would lift me from the weary life of a common shellback to the life of ease that had been mine during my early years. I tell you, in that instant, as I staggered almost blindly out of that dark little apartment, I had no thought of any horror that might be held in that incredible vessel out there afloat on the wide Atlantic.

I was full of the one blinding thought that possibly I was *rich*! And I wanted to get somewhere by myself as soon as possible to see whether I was right. Also, if I could, I meant to get back to that strange cabinet of stone, if the chance came; for I knew that I had left a lot behind.

Only, whatever I did, I must let no one guess; for then I should probably lose everything, or have but an infinitesimal share doled out to me, of the wealth that I believed to be in those glittering things there in the side pocket of my coat.

I began immediately to wonder what other treasures there might be aboard; and then, abruptly, I realized that the Captain was speaking to me:

"The light, Duprey!" he was saying, angrily, in a low tone. "What's the matter with you? Hold it up!"

I pulled myself together, and shoved the lamp above my head. One of the men was swinging his ax, to beat in the door that seemed to have stood so eternally ajar; and the rest were standing back to give him some room. Crash! went the ax, and half the door fell inward, in a shower of broken stone, making dismal splashes in the darkness. The man struck again, and the rest of the door fell away with a sullen slump into the water.

"The lamp," muttered the Captain. But I had hold of myself once more, and I was stepping forward slowly through the thigh-deep water even before he spoke.

I went a couple of paces in through the black gape of the doorway, and then stopped and held the lamp so as to get a view of the place. As I did so, I remember how the intense silence struck home to me. Every man of us must surely have been holding his breath; and there must have been some heavy quality, either in the water or in the scum that floated on it, that kept it from rippling against the sides of the bulkheads, with the movements we had made.

At first, as I held the lamp (which was burning badly), I could not get its position right to show me anything except that I was in a very large cabin for so small a vessel. Then I saw that a table ran along the center, and the top of it was no more than a few inches above the water. On each side of it there rose the backs of

114

what were evidently two rows of massive, olden-looking chairs. At the far end of the table there was a huge, immobile, humped something.

I stared at this for several moments; then I took three slow steps forward, and stopped again; for the thing resolved itself, under the light from the lamp, into the figure of an enormous man, seated at the end of the table, his face bowed forward upon his arms. I was amazed, and thrilling abruptly with new fears and vague impossible thoughts. Without moving a step, I held the light nearer at arm's length. . . . The man was of stone, like everything in that extraordinary ship.

"That foot!" said the Captain's voice, suddenly cracking. "Look at that foot!" His voice sounded amazingly startling and hollow in that silence, and the words seemed to come back sharply at me from the vaguely seen bulkheads.

I whipped my light to starboard, and saw what he meant. A huge human foot was sticking up out of the water, on the right side of the table. It was enormous. I have never seen so vast a foot. And it also was of stone.

And then, as I stared, I saw that there was a great head above the water, over by the bulkhead.

"I've gone mad!" I said out loud, as I saw something else, more incredible.

"My God! Look at the hair on the head!" said the Captain. . . . "It's growing!" he called out once more.

I was looking. On the great head, there was becoming visible a huge mass of red hair that was surely and unmistakably rising up as we watched it.

"It's what I saw at the window!" I said. "It's what I saw at the window! I told you I saw it!"

"Come out of that, Duprey," said the third mate quietly.

"Let's get out of here!" muttered one of the men. Two or three of them called out the same thing; and then, in a moment, they began a mad rush up the stairway.

I stood dumb where I was. The hair rose up in a horrible living fashion on the great head, waving and moving. It rippled down over the forehead, and spread abruptly over the whole gargantuan stone face, hiding the features completely. Suddenly I swore at the thing madly, and I hove my ax at it. Then I was backing crazily for the door, slumping the scum as high as the deck beams in my fierce haste. I reached the stairs, caught at the stone rail that was modeled like a rope, and so hove myself up out of the water. I reached the little deckhouse, where I had seen the great head of hair. I jumped through the doorway out onto the decks, and I felt the night air sweet on my face. . . . Goodness! I ran forward along the decks. There was a babel of shouting in the waist of the ship, and a thudding of feet running. Some of the men were singing out to get into the boat; but the third mate was shouting that they must wait for me.

"He's coming," called someone. And then I was among them.

"Turn that lamp up, you idiot," said the Captain's voice. "This is just where we want light!"

I glanced down, and realized that my lamp was almost out. I turned it up, and it flared, and began again to dwindle.

"Those boys never filled it," I said. "They deserve to have their necks broken."

The men were literally tumbling over the side, and the Skipper was hurrying them.

"Down with you into the boat," he said to me. "Give me the lamp. I'll pass it down. Get a move on you!"

The Captain had evidently got his nerve back again. This was more like the man I knew. I handed him the lamp, and went over the side. All the rest had now gone, and the third mate was already in the stern, waiting.

As I landed on the thwart, there was a sudden, strange noise from aboard the ship—a sound as if some stone object were trundling down the sloping decks from aft. In that one moment, I got what you might truly call the "horrors." I seemed suddenly able to believe incredible possibilities.

"The stone men!" I shouted. "Jump, Captain! Jump! Jump!" The vessel seemed to roll oddly.

Abruptly, the Captain yelled out something that not one of us in the boat understood. There followed a succession of tremendous sounds aboard the ship, and I saw his shadow swing out huge against the thin mist, as he turned suddenly with the lamp. He fired twice with his revolver.

"The hair!" I shouted. "Look at the hair!"

We all saw it—the great head of red hair that we had seen grow visibly on the monstrous stone head below in the cabin. It rose above the rail, and there was a moment of intense stillness in which I heard the Captain gasping. The third mate fired six times at the thing, and I found myself fixing an oar up against the side of that abominable vessel to get aboard.

As I did so, there came one appalling crash that shook the stone ship fore and aft, and she began to cant up, and my oar slipped and fell into the boat. Then the Captain's voice screamed something in a choking fashion above us. The ship lurched forward and paused. Then another crash came, and she rocked over towards us, then away from us again. The movement away from us continued, and the round of the vessel's bottom showed vaguely. There was a smashing of glass above us, and the dim glow of light aboard vanished. Then the vessel fell clean over from us, with a giant splash. A huge wave came at us out of the night, and half filled the boat.

The boat nearly capsized, then righted and presently steadied.

"Captain!" shouted the third mate. "Captain!" But there came never a sound; only presently, out of all the night, a strange murmuring of waters.

"Captain!" the third mate shouted once more; but his voice just went lost and remote into the darkness.

"She's foundered!" I said.

"Out oars," sang out the third mate. "Put your backs into it.

117

Don't stop to bail!"

For half an hour we circled the spot slowly. But the strange vessel had indeed foundered and gone down into the mystery of the deep sea with her mysteries.

Finally we put about and returned to the *Alfred Jessop*.

Now, I want you to realize that what I am telling you is a plain and simple tale of fact. This is no fairy tale, and I've not done yet; and I think this yarn should prove to you that some mighty strange things do happen at sea, and always will while the world lasts. It's the home of all the mysteries; for it's the one place that is really difficult for humans to investigate. Now just listen:

The mate had kept the bell going from time to time, and so we came back pretty quickly, having, as we came, a strange repetition of the echoey reduplication of our oar sounds. But we never spoke a word, for not one of us wanted to hear those beastly echoes again after what we had just gone through. I think we all had a feeling that there was something a bit hellish abroad that night.

We got aboard, and the third mate explained to the mate what had happened; but he would hardly believe the yarn. However, there was nothing to do but wait for daylight, so we were told to keep about the deck, and keep our eyes and ears open.

One thing the mate did showed he was more impressed by our yarn than he would admit. He had all the ship's lanterns lashed up around the decks to the sheerpoles, and he never told us to give up either the axes or the cutlass.

It was while we were keeping about the decks that I took the chance to have a look at what I had grabbed. I tell you, what I found made me nearly forget the Skipper and all the rummy things that had happened. I had twenty-six stones in my pocket and four of them were diamonds, respectively, 9, 11, 13½ and 17 carats in weight—uncut, that is. I know quite something about diamonds. I'm not going to tell you how I learned what I know; but I would not have taken a thousand pounds for the four as they lay there in my hand. There was also a big dull stone that looked red inside. I'd have dumped it over the side, I thought so little of it; only I argued that it must be something, or it would never have been among that lot. Lord! but I little knew what I'd got, not then. Why, the thing was as big as a fair-sized walnut. You may think it funny that I thought of the four diamonds first; but you see, I *know* diamonds when I see them. They're things I understand; but I never saw a ruby in the rough before or since. Good Lord! And to think I'd have thought nothing of heaving it over the side!

You see, a lot of the stones were not anything much; that is, not in the modern market. There were two big topaz, and several onyx and cornelians—nothing much. There were five hammered slugs of gold about two ounces each. And then a prize—one winking green devil of an emerald. You've got to know an emerald to look for the "eye" of it in the rough; but it is there—the eye of some hidden devil staring up at you. Yes, I'd seen an emerald before, and I knew I held a lot of money in that one stone alone.

And then I remembered what I'd missed, and cursed myself for not grabbing a third time. But that feeling lasted only a moment. I thought of the beastly part that had been the Skipper's share while there I stood safe under one of the lamps, with a fortune in my hands. And then, abruptly, as you can understand, my mind was filled with the crazy wonder and bewilderment of what had happened. I felt how absurdly ineffectual my imagination was to comprehend anything understandable out of it all, except that the Captain had certainly gone, and I had just as certainly had a piece of impossible luck.

Often, during that time of waiting, I stopped to take a look at the things I had in my pocket, always careful that no one about the decks should come near me to see what I was looking at.

Suddenly the mate's voice came sharp along the decks:

"Call the doctor, one of you," he said. "Tell him to get the fire in and the coffee made."

"Aye, sir," said one of the men, and I realized that the dawn was growing vaguely over the sea.

Half an hour later, the "doctor" shoved his head out of the galley doorway and sang out that coffee was ready.

The watch below turned out, and had theirs with the watch on deck, all sitting along the spar that lay under the port rail.

As the daylight grew, we kept a constant watch over the side; but even now we could see nothing, for the thin mist still hung low on the sea.

"Hear that?" said one of the men suddenly. And, indeed, the sound must have been plain for half a mile around.

"Ooaaze, ooaaze, arrr, arrrr, oooaze ———"

"By George!" said Tallett, one of the other watch; "that's a beastly sort of thing to hear."

"Look!" I said. "What's that out yonder?"

The mist was thinning under the effect of the rising sun, and tremendous shapes seemed to stand towering, half-seen, away to port. A few minutes passed while we stared. Then, suddenly, we heard the mate's voice:

"All hands on deck!" he was shouting along the decks.

I ran aft a few steps.

"Both watches are out, sir," I called.

"Very good!" said the mate. "Keep handy, all of you. Some of you have got the axes. The rest had better take a caps'n'bar each, and stand by till I find what this devilment is out yonder."

"Aye, aye, sir," I said, and turned forrard. But there was no need to pass on the mate's orders; for the men had heard, and there was a rush for the capstanbars, which are a pretty hefty kind of cudgel, as any sailorman knows. We lined the rail again, and stared away to port.

"Look out, you sea divvils," shouted Timothy Galt, a huge Irishman, waving his bar excitedly, and peering over the rail into the mist, which was steadily thinning as the day grew.

Abruptly there was a simultaneous cry. "*Rocks!*" shouted everyone.

I never saw such a sight. As at last the mist thinned, we could

120

see them. All the sea to port was literally cut about with far-reaching reefs of rock. In places the reefs lay just submerged, but in others they rose into extraordinary and fantastic rock spires and arches and islands of jagged rock.

"Jehosaphat!" I heard the third mate shout. "Look at that, Mister! Look at that! Lord! How did we take the boat through that without stoving her!"

Everything was so still for the moment, with all the men just staring and amazed, that I could hear every word come along the decks.

"There's sure been a submarine earthquake somewhere," I heard the first mate say. "The bottom of the sea's just riz up here, quiet and gentle, during the night; and God's mercy we aren't now atop one of those ornaments out there."

And then, you know, I saw it all. Everything that had looked mad and impossible began to be natural; though it was, none the less, all amazing and wonderful.

There had been, during the night, a slow lifting of the sea bottom owing to some action of the Internal Pressures. The rocks had risen so gently that they had made never a sound, and the stone ship had risen with them out of the deep sea. She had evidently lain on one of the submerged reefs, and so had seemed to us to be just afloat in the sea. And she accounted for the water we heard running. She was naturally hung full, as you might say, and took longer to shed the water than she did to rise. She had probably some biggish holes in her bottom. I began to get my "soundings" a bit, as I might call it in sailor talk. The natural wonders of the sea beat all made-up yarns that ever were!

The mate sang out to us to man the boat again, and told the third mate to take her out to where we lost the Skipper, and have a final look around, in case there might be any chance to find the Old Man's body anywhere about.

"Keep a man in the bows to look out for sunk rocks, Mister," the mate told the third mate, as we pulled off. "Go slow. There'll be no wind yet awhile. See if you can fix up what made those noises, while you're looking round."

We pulled right across about thirty fathoms of clear water, and in a minute we were between two great arches of rock. It was then I realized that the reduplicating of our oar roll was the echo from these on each side of us. Even in the sunlight, it was queer to hear again that same strange cathedral echoey sound that we had heard in the dark.

We passed under the huge arches, all hung with deep-sea slime. And presently we were heading straight for a gap where two low reefs swept in to the apex of a huge horseshoe. We pulled for about three minutes, and then the third mate gave the word to vast pulling.

"Take the boat hook, Duprey," he said, "and go forrard, and see we don't hit anything."

"Aye, aye, sir," I said, and drew in my oar.

"Give way again gently!" said the third mate; and the boat moved forward for another thirty or forty yards.

"We're right on to a reef, sir," I said presently, as I stared down over the bows. I sounded with the boat hook. "There's about three feet of water, sir," I told him.

"Vast pulling," ordered the third mate. "I reckon we are right over the rock where we found that rum packet last night." He leaned over the side and stared down.

"There's a stone cannon on the rock, right under the bows of the boat," I said. Immediately afterwards I shouted:

"There's the hair, sir! There's the hair! It's on the reef. There's two! There's three! There's one on the cannon!"

"All right! All right, Duprey! Keep cool," said the third mate. "I can see them. You've enough intelligence not to be superstitious now the whole thing's explained. They're some kind of big hairy sea-caterpillar. Prod one with your boat hook."

I did so, a little ashamed of my sudden bewilderment. The thing whipped around like a tiger at the boat hook. It lapped itself round

122

and round the boat hook, while the hind portions of it kept gripped to the rock. I could no more pull the boat hook from its grip than fly, though I pulled till I sweated.

"Take the point of your cutlass to it, Varley," said the third mate. "Jab it through."

The bow oar did so, and the brute loosed the boat hook, and curled up around a chunk of rock, looking like a great ball of red hair.

I drew the boat hook up and examined it.

"Goodness!" I said. "That's what killed the Old Man—one of those things! Look at all those marks in the wood, where it's gripped it with about a hundred legs."

I passed the boat hook aft to the third mate to look at.

"They're about as dangerous as they can be, sir, I reckon," I told him. "Makes you think of African centipedes, only these are big and strong enough to kill an elephant, I should think."

"Don't lean all on one side of the boat!" shouted the third mate, as the men stared over. "Get back to your places. Give way, there! . . . Keep a good lookout for any signs of the ship or the Captain, Duprey."

For nearly an hour we pulled to and fro over the reef; but we never saw either the stone ship or the Old Man again. The queer craft must have rolled off into the profound depths that lay on each side of the reef.

As I leaned over the bows, staring down all that long while at the submerged rocks, I was able to understand almost everything, except the various extraordinary noises.

The cannon made it unmistakably clear that the ship which had been hove up from the sea bottom, with the rising of the reef, had been originally a normal enough wooden vessel of a time far removed from our own. At the sea bottom, she had evidently undergone some natural mineralizing process, and this explained her stony appearance. The stone men had evidently been humans who had been drowned in her cabin, and their swollen tissues had been subjected to the same natural process, which, however, had also deposited heavy encrustations upon them, so that their size, when compared with the normal, was prodigious.

The mystery of the hair I had already discovered; but there remained, among other things, the tremendous bangs we had heard. These were, possibly, explained later, while we were making a final examination of the rocks to the westward, prior to returning to our ship. Here we discovered the burst and swollen bodies of several extraordinary deep-sea creatures of the eel variety. They must have had a girth, in life, of many feet, and one that we measured roughly with an oar must have been quite forty feet long. They had, apparently, burst on being lifted from the tremendous pressure of the deep sea into the light air pressure above water, and hence might account for the loud reports we had heard; though, personally, I incline to think these loud bangs were more probably caused by the splitting of the rocks under new stresses.

As for the roaring sounds, I can only conclude that they were caused by a peculiar species of grampus-like fish of enormous size which we found dead and hugely distended on one of the rocky masses. This fish must have weighed at least four or five tons, and when prodded with a heavy oar there came from its peculiar snout-shaped mouth a low, hoarse sound, like a weak imitation of the tremendous sounds we had heard during the past night.

Regarding the apparently carved handrail, like a rope up the side of the cabin stairs, I realize that this had undoubtedly been actual rope at one time.

Recalling the heavy, trundling sounds aboard, just after I climbed down into the boat, I can only suppose that these were made by some stone object, possibly a fossilized gun carriage, rolling down the decks as the ship began to slip off the rocks and her bows sank lower in the water.

The varying lights must have been the strongly phosphorescent bodies of some of the deep-sea creatures moving about on the upheaved reefs. As for the giant splash that occurred in the darkness ahead of the boat, this must have been due to some large portion of heaved-up rock overbalancing and rolling back into the sea.

No one aboard ever learned about the jewels. I took care of that! I sold the ruby badly, so I've heard since, but I do not grumble even now. Twenty-three thousand pounds I had for it alone, from a merchant in London. I learned afterwards he made double that on it; but I don't spoil my pleasure by grumbling. I wonder often how the stones and things came where I found them; but she carried guns, as I've told, I think; and there's rum doings happen at sea; yes, by George!

The smell—oh that, I guess, was due to heaving all that deep-sea slime up for human noses to smell at.

This yarn is, of course, known in nautical circles, and was briefly mentioned in the old Nautical Mercury of 1879. The series of volcanic reefs (which disappeared in 1883) were charted under the name of the "Alfred Jessop Shoals and Reefs"; being named after our Captain who discovered them and lost his life on them.

Forty Singing Seamen

ALFRED NOYES

Across the seas of Wonderland to Mogadore we plodded,
Forty singing seamen in an old black barque,
And we landed in the twilight where a Polyphemus nodded,
With his battered moon-eye winking red and yellow through the
    dark!
  For his eye was growing mellow,
  Rich and ripe and red and yellow,
As was time, since old Ulysses made him bellow in the dark!
Since Ulysses bunged his eye up with a pine-torch in the dark!

Were they mountains in the gloaming or the giant's ugly shoulders
Just beneath the rolling eye-ball, with its bleared and vinous glow,
Red and yellow o'er the purple of the pines among the boulders
And the shaggy horror brooding on the sullen slopes below,
Were they pines among the boulders
  Or the hair upon his shoulders?
We were only simple seamen, so of course we didn't know.
We were simple singing seamen, so of course we couldn't know.

But we crossed a plain of poppies, and we came upon a fountain
Not of water, but of jewels, like a spray of leaping fire;
And behind it, in an emerald glade, beneath a golden mountain
There stood a crystal palace, for a sailor to admire;
  For a troop of ghosts came round us,
  Which with leaves of bay they crowned us,

Then with grog they well-nigh drowned us, to the depth of our
    desire!
And 'twas very friendly of them, as a sailor can admire!

There was music all about us, we were growing quite forgetful
We were only singing seamen from the dirt of London-town,
Though the nectar that we swallowed seemed to vanish half
    regretful
As if we wasn't good enough to take such vittles down,
    When we saw a sudden figure,
Like the devil—only bigger—drawing near us with a frown!
Like the devil—but much bigger—and he wore a golden crown!

And "What's all this?" he growls at us! With dignity we chaunted,
"Forty singing seamen, sir, as won't be put upon!"
"What? Englishmen?" he cries, "Well, if ye don't mind being
    haunted,
Faith, you're welcome to my palace; I'm the famous Prester John!
    Will ye walk into my palace?
    I don't bear 'ee any malice!
One and all ye shall be welcome in the halls of Prester John!"
So we walked into the palace and the halls of Prester John!

Now the door was one great diamond and the hall a hollow ruby—
Big as Beachy Head, my lads, nay, bigger by a half!
And I sees the mate wi' mouth agape, a-staring like a booby,
And the skipper close behind him, with his tongue out like a calf!
    Now the way to take it rightly
    Was to walk along politely
Just as if you didn't notice—so I couldn't help but laugh!
For they both forgot their manners and the crew was bound to
    laugh!

But he took us through his palace, and, my lads, as I'm a sinner,
We walked into an opal like a sunset-colored cloud—
"My dining room," he says, and, quick as light, we saw a dinner
Spread before us by the fingers of a hidden fairy crowd;
   And the skipper, swaying gently
   After dinner, murmurs faintly,
"I looks to-wards you, Prester John, you've done us very proud!"
And he drank his health with honors, for he *done* us *very* proud!

Then he walks us to his gardens where we sees a feathered demon
Very splendid and important on a sort of spicy tree!
"That's the Phoenix," whispers Prester, "which all eddicated sea-
    men
Knows the only one existent, and he's waiting for to flee!
   When his hundred years expire
   Then he'll set hisself a-fire
And another from his ashes rise most beautiful to see!
With wings of rose and emerald most beautiful to see!"

Then he says, "In yonder forest there's a little silver river
And whosoever drinks of it, his youth will never die!
The centuries go by, but Prester John endures for ever
With his music in the mountains and his magic on the sky!
   While *your* hearts are growing colder,
   While your world is growing older,
There's a magic in the distance, where the sea-line meets the sky.
It shall call to singing seamen till the fount o' song is dry!"

So we thought we'd up and seek it, but that forest fair defied us,—
First a crimson leopard laughed at us most horrible to see,
Then a sea-green lion came and sniffed and licked his chops and
    eyed us,
While a red and yellow unicorn was dancing round a tree!
   We was trying to look thinner,

Which was hard, because our dinner
Must ha' made us very tempting to a cat o' high degree!
Must ha' made us very tempting to the whole menarjeree!

So we scuttled from that forest and across the poppy meadows
Where the awful shaggy horror brooded o'er us in the dark!
And we pushes out from shore again a-jumping at our shadows
And pulls away most joyful to the old black barque!
    And home again we plodded

While the Polyphemus nodded
With his battered moon-eye winking red and yellow through the
dark.
Oh, the moon above the mountains red and yellow through the
dark!

Across the seas of Wonderland to London-town we blundered,
Forty singing seamen as was puzzled for to know
If the visions that we saw was caused by—here again we pon-
dered—
A tipple in a vision forty thousand years ago.
Could the grog we *dreamt* we swallowed
Make us *dream* of all that followed?
We were simply singing seamen, so of course we didn't know!
We were simply singing seamen, so of course we could not know!

Perhaps there are still islands of mystery and danger waiting to be discovered in some distant sea—islands, maybe, like this one.

The Voice in the Night

WILLIAM HOPE HODGSON

It was a dark, starless night. We were becalmed in the Northern Pacific. Our exact position I do not know; for the sun had been hidden, during the course of a weary, breathless week, by a thin haze which had seemed to float above us, about the height of our mastheads, at whiles descending and shrouding the surrounding sea.

With there being no wind, we had steadied the tiller, and I was the only man on deck. The crew, consisting of two men and a boy, were sleeping forward in their den; while Will—my friend, and the master of our little craft—was aft in his bunk on the port side of the little cabin.

Suddenly, from out of the surrounding darkness, there came a hail: "Schooner, ahoy!"

The cry was so unexpected that I gave no immediate answer, because of my surprise.

It came again—a voice curiously throaty and inhuman, calling from somewhere upon the dark sea away on our port broadside.

"Schooner, ahoy!"

"Hullo!" I sang out, having gathered my wits somewhat. "What are you? What do you want?"

"You need not be afraid," answered the queer voice, having probably noticed some trace of confusion in my tone. "I am only an old—man."

The pause sounded oddly; but it was only afterward that it came back to me with any significance.

"Why don't you come alongside, then?" I queried somewhat snappishly; for I liked not his hinting at my having been a trifle shaken.

"I—I—can't. It wouldn't be safe. I—" The voice broke off, and there was silence.

"What do you mean?" I asked, growing more and more astonished. "What would not be safe? Where are you?"

I listened for a moment; but there came no answer. And then, a sudden indefinite suspicion of I knew not what coming to me, I stepped swiftly to the binnacle, and took out the lighted lamp. At the same time, I knocked on the deck with my heel to waken Will. Then I was back at the side, throwing the yellow funnel of light out into the silent immensity beyond our rail. As I did so, I heard a slight, muffled cry, and then the sound of a splash as though some-one had dipped oars abruptly. Yet I cannot say that I saw anything with certainty; save, it seemed to me, that in the first flash of the light, there had been something upon the waters, where now there was nothing.

"Hullo, there!" I called. "What foolery is this!"

But there came only the indistinct sounds of a boat being pulled away into the night.

Then I heard Will's voice, from the direction of the after scuttle.

134

"What's up, George?"

"Come here, Will!" I said.

"What is it?" he asked, coming across the deck.

I told him the queer thing which had happened. He put several questions; then, after a moment's silence, he raised his hands to his lips and hailed, "Boat, ahoy!"

From a long distance away there came back to us a faint reply, and my companion repeated his call. Presently, after a short period of silence, there grew on our hearing the muffled sound of oars; at which Will hailed again.

This time there was a reply. "Put away the light."

Will told me to do as the voice bade, and I shoved it down under the bulwarks.

"Come nearer," he said, and the oar strokes continued. Then, when apparently some half-dozen fathoms distant, they again ceased.

"Come alongside," exclaimed Will. "There's nothing to be frightened of aboard here!"

"Promise that you will not show the light?"

"What's to do with you," I burst out, "that you're so infernally afraid of the light?"

"Because—" began the voice, and stopped short.

"Because what?" I asked quickly.

Will put his hand on my shoulder. "Shut up a minute, old man," he said in a low voice. "Let me tackle him."

He leaned more over the rail.

"See here, mister," he said, "this is a pretty queer business, you coming upon us like this, right out in the middle of the blessed Pacific. How are we to know what sort of a hanky-panky trick you're up to? You say there's only one of you. How are we to know, unless we get a squint at you—eh? What's your objection to the light, anyway?"

As he finished, I heard the noise of the oars again, and then the voice came; but now from a greater distance, and sounding extremely hopeless and pathetic.

"I am sorry—sorry! I would not have troubled you, only I am hungry, and—so is she."

The voice died away, and the sound of the oars, dipping irregularly, was borne to us.

"Stop!" sang out Will. "I don't want to drive you away. Come back! We'll keep the light hidden, if you don't like it."

He turned to me. "It's a queer rig, this; but I think there's nothing to be afraid of?"

There was a question in his tone, and I replied. "No, I think the poor devil's been wrecked around here, and gone crazy."

The sound of the oars drew nearer.

"Shove that lamp back in the binnacle," said Will; then he leaned over the rail and listened. I replaced the lamp, and came back to his side. The dipping of the oars ceased some dozen yards distant.

"Won't you come alongside now?" asked Will in an even voice. "I have had the lamp put back in the binnacle."

"I—I cannot," replied the voice. "I dare not come nearer. I dare not even pay you for the—the provisions."

"That's all right," said Will, and hesitated. "You're welcome to as much grub as you can take—" Again he hesitated.

"You are very good," exclaimed the voice. "May God, Who understands everything, reward you—" It broke off huskily.

"The—the lady?" said Will abruptly. "Is she—"

"I have left her behind upon the island," came the voice.

"What island?" I cut in.

"I know not its name," returned the voice. "I would to God—!" it began, and checked itself as suddenly.

"Could we not send a boat for her?" asked Will at this point.

"No!" said the voice, with extraordinary emphasis. "My God! No!" There was a moment's pause; then it added, in a tone which seemed a merited reproach, "It was because of our want I ventured—because her agony tortured me."

136

"I am a forgetful brute," exclaimed Will. "Just wait a minute, whoever you are, and I will bring you up something at once."

In a couple of minutes he was back again, and his arms were full of various edibles. He paused at the rail.

"Can't you come alongside for them?" he asked.

"No—I *dare not*," replied the voice, and it seemed to me that in its tones I detected a note of stifled craving—as though the owner hushed a mortal desire. It came to me then in a flash that the poor old creature out there in the darkness was *suffering* for actual need of that which Will held in his arms; and yet, because of some unintelligible dread, refraining from dashing to the side of our schooner and receiving it. And with the lightning-like conviction, there came the knowledge that the Invisible was not mad, but sanely facing some intolerable horror.

"Will!" I said, full of many feelings, over which predominated a vast sympathy. "Get a box. We must float off the stuff to him in it."

This we did—propelling it away from the vessel, out into the darkness, by means of a boat hook. In a minute, a slight cry from the Invisible came to us, and we knew that he had secured the box.

A little later he called out a farewell to us, and so heartful a blessing that I am sure we were the better for it. Then, without more ado, we heard the ply of oars across the darkness.

"Pretty soon off," remarked Will, with perhaps just a little sense of injury.

"Wait," I replied. "I think somehow he'll come back. He must have been badly needing that food."

"And the lady," said Will. For a moment he was silent; then he continued, "It's the queerest thing ever I've stumbled across since I've been fishing."

"Yes," I said, and fell to pondering.

And so the time slipped away—an hour, another, and still Will stayed with me; for the queer adventure had knocked all desire for sleep out of him.

The third hour was three parts through when we heard again

the sound of oars across the silent ocean.

"Listen!" said Will, a low note of excitement in his voice.

"He's coming, just as I thought," I muttered.

The dipping of the oars grew nearer, and I noted that the strokes were firmer and longer. The food had been needed.

They came to a stop a little distance off the broadside, and the queer voice came again to us through the darkness.

"Schooner, ahoy!"

"That you?" asked Will.

"Yes," replied the voice. "I left you suddenly; but—but there was great need."

"The lady?" questioned Will.

"The—lady is grateful now on earth. She will be more grateful soon in—in heaven."

Will began to make some reply, in a puzzled voice, but became confused, and broke off short. I said nothing. I was wondering at the curious pauses, and, apart from my wonder, I was full of a great sympathy.

The voice continued. "We—she and I, have talked, as we shared the result of God's tenderness and yours—"

Will interposed; but without coherence.

"I beg of you not to—to belittle your deed of Christian charity this night," said the voice. "Be sure that it has not escaped His notice."

It stopped, and there was a full minute's silence. Then it came again.

"We have spoken together upon that which—which has befallen us. We had thought to go out, without telling anybody of the terror which has come into our—lives. She is with me in believing that tonight's happenings are under a special ruling, and that it is God's wish that we should tell to you all that we have suffered since—since—"

"Yes?" said Will softly.

"Since the sinking of the *Albatross.*"

138

"Ah!" I exclaimed involuntarily. "She left Newcastle for 'Frisco some six months ago, and hasn't been heard of since."

"Yes," answered the voice. "But some few degrees to the north of the line she was caught in a terrible storm, and dismasted. When the day came, it was found that she was leaking badly, and presently, it falling to a calm, the sailors took to the boats, leaving—leaving a young lady—my fiancée—and myself upon the wreck.

"We were below, gathering together a few of our belongings, when they left. They were entirely callous, through fear, and when we came up on the decks, we saw them only as small shapes afar off upon the horizon. Yet we did not despair, but set to work and constructed a small raft. Upon this we put such few matters as it would hold, including a quantity of water and some ship's biscuit. Then, the vessel being very deep in the water, we got ourselves on to the raft, and pushed off.

"It was later when I observed that we seemed to be in the way of some tide or current which bore us from the ship at an angle; so that in the course of three hours, by my watch, her hull became invisible to our sight, her broken masts remaining in view for a somewhat longer period. Then, toward evening, it grew misty, and so through the night. The next day we were still encompassed by the mist, the weather remaining quiet.

"For four days we drifted through this strange haze, until, on the evening of the fourth day, there grew upon our ears the murmur of breakers at a distance. Gradually it became plainer, and, somewhat after midnight, it appeared to sound upon either hand at no very great space. The raft was raised upon a swell several times, and then we were in smooth water, and the noise of the breakers was behind.

"When the morning came, we found that we were in a sort of great lagoon; but of this we noticed little at the time; for close before us, through the enshrouding mist, loomed the hull of a large sailing vessel. With one accord, we fell upon our knees and thanked God; for we thought that here was an end to our perils. We had much to learn.

"The raft drew near to the ship, and we shouted at them to take us aboard; but none answered. Presently the raft touched against the side of the vessel, and, seeing a rope hanging downward, I seized it and began to climb. Yet I had much ado to make my way up, because of a kind of gray, lichenous fungus which had seized upon the rope, and which blotched the side of the ship lividly.

"I reached the rail and clambered over it, on to the deck. Here I saw that the decks were covered, in great patches, with the gray masses, some of them rising into nodules several feet in height; but at the time I thought less of this matter than of the possibility of there being people aboard the ship. I shouted; but none answered. Then I went to the door below the poop deck. I opened it, and peered in. There was a great smell of staleness, so that I knew in a moment that nothing living was within, and with the knowledge, I shut the door quickly; for I felt suddenly lonely.

"I went back to the side where I had scrambled up. My—my sweetheart was still sitting quietly upon the raft. Seeing me look down, she called up to know whether there were any people aboard the ship. I replied that the vessel had the appearance of having been long deserted; but that if she would wait a little I would see whether there was anything in the shape of a ladder by which she could ascend to the deck. Then we would make a search through the vessel together. A little later, on the opposite side of the decks, I found a rope side ladder. This I carried across, and a minute afterward she was beside me.

"Together we explored the cabins and apartments in the after part of the ship; but nowhere was there any sign of life. Here and there, within the cabins themselves, we came across odd patches of that queer fungus; but this, as my sweetheart said, could be cleansed away.

"In the end, having assured ourselves that the after portion of the vessel was empty, we picked our way to the bows, between the ugly gray nodules of that strange growth; and here we made a

140

further search, which told us that there was indeed none aboard but ourselves.

"This being now beyond any doubt, we returned to the stern of the ship and proceeded to make ourselves as comfortable as possible. Together we cleared out and cleaned two of the cabins; and after that I made examination whether there was anything eatable in the ship. This I soon found was so, and thanked God in my heart for His goodness. In addition to this I discovered the whereabouts of the fresh-water pump, and having fixed it I found the water drinkable, though somewhat unpleasant to the taste.

"For several days we stayed aboard the ship, without attempting to get to the shore. We were busily engaged in making the place habitable. Yet even thus early we became aware that our lot was even less to be desired than might have been imagined; for though, as a first step, we scraped away the odd patches of growth that studded the floors and walls of the cabins and saloon, they returned almost to their original size within the space of twenty-four hours, which not only discouraged us, but gave us a feeling of vague unease.

"Still we would not admit ourselves beaten, so set to work afresh, and not only scraped away the fungus, but soaked the places where it had been, with carbolic, a canful of which I had found in the pantry. Yet, by the end of the week the growth had returned in full strength, and, in addition it had spread to other places, as though our touching it had allowed germs from it to travel elsewhere.

"On the seventh morning, my sweetheart woke to find a small patch of it growing on her pillow, close to her face. At that, she came to me, as soon as she could get her garments upon her. I was in the galley at the time lighting the fire for breakfast.

" 'Come here, John,' she said, and led me aft. When I saw the thing upon her pillow I shuddered, and then and there we agreed to go right out of the ship and see whether we could not fare to make ourselves more comfortable ashore.

"Hurriedly we gathered together our few belongings, and even

141

among these I found that the fungus had been at work; for one of her shawls had a little lump of it growing near one edge. I threw the whole thing over the side, without saying anything to her.

"The raft was still alongside, but it was too clumsy to guide, and I lowered down a small boat that hung across the stern, and in this we made our way to the shore. Yet, as we drew near to it, I became gradually aware that here the vile fungus, which had driven us from the ship, was growing riot. In places it rose into horrible, fantastic mounds, which seemed almost to quiver, as with a quiet life, when the wind blew across them. Here and there it took on the forms of vast fingers, and in others it just spread out flat and smooth and treacherous. Odd places, it appeared as grotesque stunted trees, seeming extraordinarily kinked and gnarled—the whole quaking vilely at times.

"At first, it seemed to us that there was no single portion of the surrounding shore which was not hidden beneath the masses of the hideous lichen; yet, in this, I found we were mistaken; for somewhat later, coasting along the shore at a little distance, we descried a smooth white patch of what appeared to be fine sand, and there we landed. It was not sand. What it was I do not know. All that I have observed is that upon it the fungus will not grow; while everywhere else, save where the sandlike earth wanders oddly, pathwise, amid the gray desolation of the lichen, there is nothing but that loathsome grayness.

"It is difficult to make you understand how cheered we were to find one place that was absolutely free from the growth, and here we deposited our belongings. Then we went back to the ship for such things as it seemed to us we should need. Among other matters, I managed to bring ashore with me one of the ship's sails, with which I constructed two small tents. Though exceedingly rough shaped, they served the purposes for which they were intended. In these we lived and stored our various necessities, and thus for a matter of some four weeks all went smoothly and without particular unhappiness. Indeed, I may say with much of happiness—for—we were together.

"It was on the thumb of her right hand that the growth first showed. It was only a small circular spot, much like a little gray mole. My God! how the fear leaped to my heart when she showed me the place. We cleansed it, between us, washing it with carbolic and water. In the morning of the following day she showed her hand to me again. The gray warty thing had returned. For a little while, we looked at one another in silence. Then, still wordless, we started again to remove it. In the midst of the operation she spoke suddenly.

" 'What's that on the side of your face, dear?' Her voice was sharp with anxiety. I put my hand up to feel.

" 'There! Under the hair by your ear. A little to the front a bit.' My finger rested upon the place, and then I knew.

" 'Let us get your thumb done first,' I said. And she submitted, only because she was afraid to touch me until it was cleansed. I finished washing and disinfecting her thumb, and then she turned to my face. After it was finished we sat together and talked awhile of many things; for there had come into our lives sudden, very terrible thoughts. We were, all at once, afraid of something worse than death. We spoke of loading the boat with provisions and water and making our way out onto the sea; yet we were helpless, for many causes, and—and the growth had attacked us already. We decided to stay. God would do with us what was His will. We would wait.

"A month, two months, three months passed, and the places grew somewhat, and there had come others. Yet we fought so strenuously with the fear that its headway was but slow, comparatively speaking.

"Occasionally we ventured off to the ship for such stores as we needed. There we found that the fungus grew persistently. One of the nodules on the main deck became soon as high as my head.

"We had now given up all thought or hope of leaving the island. We had realized that it would be unallowable to go among healthy humans, with the thing from which we were suffering.

"With this determination and knowledge in our minds we knew that we should have to husband our food and water; for we did not know, at that time, but that we should possibly live for many years.

"This reminds me that I have told you that I am an old man. Judged by years this is not so. But—but—"

He broke off; then continued somewhat abruptly.

"As I was saying, we knew that we should have to use care in the matter of food. But we had no idea then how little food there was left, of which to take care. It was a week later that I made the discovery that all the other bread tanks—which I had supposed full—were empty, and that (beyond odd tins of vegetables and meat, and some other matters) we had nothing on which to depend but the bread in the tank which I had already opened.

"After learning this I bestirred myself to do what I could, and set to work at fishing in the lagoon; but with no success. At this I was somewhat inclined to feel desperate until the thought came to me to try outside the lagoon, in the open sea.

"Here, at times, I caught odd fish; but so infrequently that they proved of but little help in keeping us from the hunger which threatened. It seemed to me that our deaths were likely to come by hunger, and not by the growth of the thing which had seized upon our bodies.

"We were in this state of mind when the fourth month wore out. Then I made a very horrible discovery. One morning, a little before midday, I came off from the ship with a portion of the biscuits which were left. In the mouth of her tent I saw my sweetheart sitting, eating something.

"'What is it, my dear?' I called out as I leaped ashore. Yet, on hearing my voice, she seemed confused, and, turning, slyly threw something toward the edge of the little clearing. It fell short, and a vague suspicion having arisen within me, I walked across and picked it up. It was a piece of the gray fungus.

"As I went to her with it in my hand, she turned deadly pale;

then a rose red.

"I felt strangely dazed and frightened.

" 'My dear! My dear!' I said, and could say no more. Yet at my words she broke down and cried bitterly. Gradually, as she calmed, I got from her the news that she had tried it the preceding day, and—and liked it. I got her to promise on her knees not to touch it again, however great our hunger. After she had promised she told me that the desire for it had come suddenly, and that, until the moment of desire, she had experienced nothing toward it but the most extreme repulsion.

"Later in the day, feeling strangely restless, and much shaken with the thing which I had discovered, I made my way along one of the twisted paths—formed by the white, sandlike substance—which led among the fungoid growth. I had, once before, ventured along there; but not to any great distance. This time, being involved in perplexing thought, I went much further than hitherto.

"Suddenly I was called to myself by a queer hoarse sound on my left. Turning quickly, I saw there was movement among an extraordinarily shaped mass of fungus, close to my elbow. It was swaying uneasily, as though it possessed life of its own. Abruptly, as I stared, the thought came to me that the thing had a grotesque resemblance to the figure of a distorted human creature. Even as the fancy flashed into my brain, there was a slight, sickening noise of tearing, and I saw that one of the branchlike arms was detaching itself from the surrounding gray masses, and coming toward me. The head of the thing—a shapeless gray ball, inclined in my direction. I stood stupidly, and the vile arm brushed across my face. I gave out a frightened cry, and ran back a few paces. There was a sweetish taste upon my lips where the thing had touched me. I licked them, and was immediately filled with an inhuman desire. I turned and seized a mass of the fungus. Then more, and—more. I was insatiable. In the midst of devouring, the remembrance of the morning's discovery swept into my amazed brain. It was sent by God. I dashed the fragment I held to the ground. Then, utterly

wretched and feeling a dreadful guiltiness, I made my way back
to the little encampment.

"I think she knew, by some marvelous intuition which love must
have given, as soon as she set eyes on me. Her quiet sympathy made
it easier for me, and I told her of my sudden weakness; yet I
omitted to mention the extraordinary thing which had gone before.
I desired to spare her all unnecessary terror.

"But, for myself, I had added an intolerable knowledge, to
breed an incessant terror in my brain; for I doubted not but that
I had seen the end of one of these men who had come to the island
in the ship in the lagoon; and in that monstrous ending I had seen
our own.

"Thereafter we kept from the abominable food, though the
desire for it had entered into our blood. Yet our drear punishment
was upon us; for, day by day, with monstrous rapidity, the fungoid
growth took hold of our poor bodies. Nothing we could do would
check it materially, and so—and so—we who had been human,
became— Well, it matters less each day. Only—only we had been
man and maid!

"And day by day the fight is more dreadful, to withstand the
hunger-lust for the terrible lichen.

"A week ago we ate the last of the biscuit, and since that time I
have caught three fish. I was out here fishing tonight when your
schooner drifted upon me out of the mist. I hailed you. You know
the rest, and may God, out of His great heart, bless you for your
goodness to a—a couple of poor outcast souls."

There was the dip of an oar—another. Then the voice came
again, and for the last time, sounding through the slight surround-
ing mist, ghostly and mournful.

"God bless you! Good by!"

"Good by," we shouted together, hoarsely, our hearts full of
many emotions.

I glanced about me. I became aware that the dawn was upon us.
The sun flung a stray beam across the hidden sea, pierced the

146

mist dully, and lit up the receding boat with a gloomy fire. Indistinctly I saw something nodding between the oars. I thought of a sponge—a great, gray nodding sponge— The oars continued to ply. They were gray—as was the boat—and my eyes searched a moment vainly for the conjunction of hand and oar. My gaze flashed back to the—head. It nodded forward as the oars went backward for the stroke. Then the oars were dipped, the boat shot out of the patch of light, and the—the thing went nodding into the mist.

The City in the Sea

EDGAR ALLAN POE

Lo! Death has reared himself a throne
In a strange city lying alone
Far down within the dim West
Where the good and the bad and the worst and the best
Have gone to their eternal rest.
There shrines and palaces and towers
(Time-eaten towers that tremble not!)
Resemble nothing that is ours.
Around, by lifting winds forgot,
Resignedly beneath the sky
The melancholy waters lie.

No rays from the holy Heaven come down
On the long night-time of that town;
But light from out the lurid sea
Streams up the turrets silently—
Gleams up the pinnacles far and free—
Up domes—up spires—up kingly halls—
Up fanes—up Babylon-like walls—
Up shadowy long-forgotten bowers
Of sculptured ivy and stone flowers—
Up many and many a marvelous shrine
Whose wreathèd friezes intertwine
The viol, the violet, and the vine.

Resignedly beneath the sky
The melancholy waters lie.
So blend the turrets and shadows there
That all seem pendulous in air,
While from a proud tower in the town
Death looks gigantically down.
There open fanes and gaping graves
Yawn level with the luminous waves;
But not the riches there that lie
In each idol's diamond eye—
Not the gayly-jewelled dead
Tempt the waters from their bed;

For no ripples curl, alas!
Along that wilderness of glass—
No swellings tell that winds may be
Upon some far-off happier sea—
No heavings hint that winds have been
On seas less hideously serene.

But lo, a stir is in the air!
The wave—there is a movement there!
As if the towers had thrust aside,
In slightly sinking, the dull tide—
As if their tops had feebly given
A void within the filmy Heaven.
The waves have now a redder glow—
The hours are breathing faint and low—
And when, amid no earthly moans,
Down, down that town shall settle hence,
Hell, rising from a thousand thrones,
Shall do it reverence.

A curse lay upon the ship and it was set to run until Dooms-
day—unless one man could manage to remove it.

The Phantom Ship

CAPTAIN FREDERICK MARRYAT

The ship had now gained off the southern coast of Africa, and was about one hundred miles from the Lagullas coast. The morning was beautiful, a slight ripple only turned the waves, the breeze was light and steady, and the vessel was standing on a wind at the rate of about four miles an hour.

But the scene was soon changed; a bank of clouds rose up from the eastward, with a rapidity that to the seamen's eyes was unnatural, and it soon covered the whole firmament; the sun was obscured, and all was one deep and unnatural gloom; the wind subsided; and the ocean was hushed. It was not exactly dark, but the heavens were covered with one red haze, which gave an appearance as if the world was in a state of conflagration.

In the cabin the increased darkness was first observed by Philip,

153

who went on deck; he was followed by the captain and passengers, who were in a state of amazement. It was unnatural and incomprehensive.

"Now, Holy Virgin, protect us! What can this be?" exclaimed the captain, in a fright. "Holy Saint Antonio, protect us! But this is awful."

"There—there!" shouted the sailors, pointing to the beam of the vessel. Every eye looked over the gunnel to witness what had occasioned such exclamations. Philip, Schriften, and the captain were side by side. On the beam of the ship, not more than two cables' length distant, they beheld slowly rising out of the water the tapering masthead and spars of another vessel. She rose, and rose, gradually; her topmasts and topsail yards, with the sails set, next made their appearance; higher and higher she rose up from the element. Her lower masts and rigging, and, lastly, her hull showed itself above the surface. Still she rose up, till her ports, with her guns, and at last the whole of her floatage was above water, and there she remained close to them, with her main yard squared, and hove to.

"Holy Virgin!" exclaimed the captain, breathless. "I have known ships to *go down,* but never to *come up* before. Now will I give one thousand candles, of ten ounces each, to the shrine of the Virgin, to save us in this trouble. One thousand wax candles! Hear me, blessed lady, ten ounces each! Gentlemen," cried the captain to the passengers, who stood aghast, "why don't you promise? Promise, I say *promise,* at all events."

"The Phantom Ship—the *Flying Dutchman,*" shrieked Schriften. "I told you so, Philip Vanderdecken. There is your father. He, he!"

Philip's eyes had remained fixed on the vessel; he perceived that they were lowering down a boat from her quarter. "It is possible," thought he, "I shall now be permitted," and he put his hand into his bosom and grasped the relic.

The gloom now increased, so that the strange vessel's hull could but just be discovered through the murky atmosphere. The seamen and passengers threw themselves down on their knees, and invoked their saints. The captain ran down for a candle, to light before the image of St. Antonio, which he took out of its shrine and kissed with much apparent affection and devotion, and then replaced.

Shortly afterwards, the splash of oars was heard alongside and a voice calling out, "I say, my good people, give us a rope from forward."

No one answered or complied with the request. Schriften went up to the captain and told him that if the strangers offered to send letters they must not be accepted or the vessel would be doomed and all would perish.

A man now made his appearance from over the gunnel, at the gangway. "You might as well have let me have a side rope, my hearties," said he, as he stepped on deck. "Where is the captain?"

"Here," replied the captain, trembling from head to foot. The man who accosted him appeared to be a weather-beaten seaman, dressed in a fur cap and canvas petticoats; he held some letters in his hand.

"What do you want?" screamed the captain at last.

"Yes—what do you want?" continued Schriften. "He! he!"

"What, you here, pilot?" observed the man. "Well—I thought you had gone to Davy's Locker long ago."

"He! he!" replied Schriften, turning away.

"Why, the fact is, captain, we have had very foul weather, and we wish to send letters home; I do believe that we shall never get around this Cape."

"I can't take them," cried the captain.

"Can't take them! Well, it's very odd, but every ship refuses to take our letters. It's very unkind; seamen should have a feeling for brother seamen, especially in distress. God knows, we wish to see our wives and families again; and it would be a matter of comfort to them if they could only hear from us."

"I cannot take your letters—the saints preserve us!" replied the captain.

"We have been a long while out," said the seaman, shaking his head.

"How long?" inquired the captain, not knowing what else to say.

"We can't tell; our almanac was blown overboard, and we have lost our reckoning. We never have our latitude exact now, for we cannot tell the sun's declination for the right day."

"Let *me* see your letters," said Philip, advancing and taking them out of the seaman's hands.

"They must not be touched," screamed Schriften.

"Out, monster!" replied Philip. "Who dares interfere with me?"

"Doomed—doomed—doomed!" shrieked Schriften, running up and down the deck, and then breaking into a wild fit of laughter.

"Touch not the letters," said the captain, trembling as if with ague.

Philip made no reply, but held his hand out for the letters.

"Here is one from our second mate to his wife at Amsterdam, who lives on Waser Quay."

"Waser Quay has long been gone, my good friend; there is now a large dock for ships where it once was," replied Philip.

"Impossible!" replied the seaman. "Here is another from myself to my sweetheart, Vrow Ketser—with money to buy her a new brooch."

Philip shook his head. "I remember seeing an old lady of that name buried some thirty years ago."

"Impossible! I left her young and blooming. Here's one for the house of Slutz and Co., to whom the ship belongs."

"There's no such house now," replied Philip, "but I have heard that, many years ago, there was a firm of that name."

"Impossible! You must be laughing at me. Here is a letter from our captain to his son ——"

"Give it to me," cried Philip, seizing the letter.

He was about to break the seal when Schriften snatched the letter out of his hand and threw it over the lee gunnel.

"That's a scurvy trick for an old shipmate," observed the seaman.

156

Schriften made no reply, but catching up the other letters which Philip had laid down on the capstan, he hurled them after the first. The strange seaman shed tears, and walked again to the side.

"It's very hard—very unkind," he observed, as he descended. "The time may come when you may wish that your family should know your situation."

So saying, he disappeared. In a few seconds we heard the sound of the oars, retreating from the ship.

"Holy Saint Antonio!" exclaimed the captain. "I am lost in wonder and fright. Steward, bring me up the arrack."

The steward ran down for the bottle; being as much alarmed as his captain, he helped himself before he brought it up to his commander.

"Now," said the captain, after keeping his mouth for two minutes to the bottle, and draining it to the bottom, "what is to be done next?"

"I'll tell you," said Schriften, going up to him. "That man there has a charm hung around his neck. Take it from him and throw it overboard, and your ship will be saved. If you do not, it will be lost, with every soul on board."

"Yes, yes, that's right, depend upon it," cried the sailors.

"Fools!" replied Philip. "Do you believe that wretch? Did you not hear the man who came on board recognize him, and call him shipmate? He is the party whose presence on board will prove so unfortunate."

"Yes, yes," cried the sailors, "that's right; the man did call him shipmate."

"I tell you it's all wrong," cried Schriften. "That is the man. Let him give up the charm."

"Yes, yes. Let him give up the charm," cried the sailors, and they rushed upon Philip.

Philip started back to where the captain stood.

"Madmen, know ye what ye are about? It is the holy cross that I wear around my neck. Throw it overboard if you dare, and your souls are lost forever." And he took the relic from his bosom and showed it to the captain.

"No, no, men," exclaimed the captain, who was now more settled in his nerves, "that won't do—the saints protect us."

The seamen, however, became clamorous; one portion were for throwing Schriften overboard, the other for throwing Philip. At last, the point was decided by the captain, who directed the small skiff hanging astern to be lowered down, and ordered both Philip and Schriften to get into it. The seamen approved of this arrangement, as it satisfied both parties. Philip made no objection; Schriften screamed and fought, but he was tossed into the boat. There he remained trembling in the stern sheets, while Philip, who had seized the sculls, pulled away from the vessel in the direction of the Phantom Ship.

In a few minutes, the vessel which Philip and Schriften had left was no longer to be discerned through the thick haze. The Phantom Ship was still in sight, but at a much greater distance from them than she was before. Philip pulled hard toward her, but although hove to, she appeared to increase her distance from the boat. For a short time he paused on his oars to regain his breath when Schriften rose up and took his seat in the stern sheets of the boat.

"You may pull and pull, Philip Vanderdecken," observed he, "but you will not gain that ship. No, no, that cannot be. We may have a long cruise together, but you will be as far from your object at the end of it, as you are now at the commencement. Why don't you throw me overboard? You would be all the lighter. He! he!"

"I felt like throwing you overboard when you attempted to force from me my relic," replied Philip.

"And have I not endeavored to make others take it from you this very day? Have I not? He! he!"

"You have," rejoined Philip, "but I am now convinced that you are as unhappy as myself, and that in what you are doing, you are only following your destiny, as I am mine. Why and wherefore I

158

cannot tell, but we are both engaged in the same mystery. If the success of my endeavors depends upon guarding the relic, the success of yours depends upon your obtaining it, and defeating my purpose by so doing. In this matter we are both agents, and you have been, so far as my mission is concerned, my most active enemy. But although you are my enemy, I *forgive you,* and will not attempt to harm you."

"You do then forgive your enemy, Philip Vanderdecken?" replied Schriften, mournfully. "For such I acknowledge myself to be."

"I do, *with all my heart, with all my soul,*" replied Philip.

"Then have you conquered me, Philip Vanderdecken. You have now made me your friend, and your wishes are about to be accomplished. You would like to know who I am. Listen. When your father, defying the Almighty's will, in his rage took my life, he was vouchsafed a chance of his doom being cancelled through the merits of his son. I had my appeal also, which was for *vengeance.* It was granted that I should remain on earth, and thwart your will. That as long as we were enemies, you should not succeed; but that when you had conformed to the highest attribute of Christianity, proved on the holy cross, that of *forgiving your enemy,* your task should be fulfilled. Philip Vanderdecken, you have forgiven your enemy, and both our destinies are now accomplished."

As Schriften spoke, Philip's eyes were fixed on him. He extended his hand to Philip—it was taken; and as it was pressed, the form of the pilot wasted as it were into the air, and Philip found himself alone.

"Father of mercy, I thank Thee," said Philip, "that my task is done."

Philip then pulled toward the Phantom Ship, and found that she no longer appeared to leave. On the contrary, every minute he was nearer and nearer, and at last he threw in his oars, climbed up her side and gained her deck.

The crew of the vessel crowded around him.

"Your captain," said Philip. "I must speak with your captain."

"Who shall I say, sir?" demanded one who appeared to be the first mate.

"Who?" replied Philip. "Tell him his son would speak to him, his son, Philip Vanderdecken."

Shouts of laughter from the crew followed this answer of Philip's, and the mate, as soon as they ceased, observed with a smile, "You forget, sir; perhaps you would say his father."

"Tell him his son, if you please," replied Philip. "Take no note of my gray hairs."

"Well, sir, here he is coming forward," replied the mate, stepping aside and pointing to the captain.

"What is all this?" inquired the captain.

"Are you Philip Vanderdecken, the captain of this vessel?"

"I am, sir," replied the other.

"You appear not to know me! But how can you? You saw me when I was only three years old."

"Ha!" replied the captain. "And who, then, are you?"

"Time has stopped with you, but with those who live in the world it stops not; and for those who pass a life of misery, it hurries on still faster. In me behold your son, Philip Vanderdecken, who after a life of such peril and misery as few have passed, has at last fulfilled his vow, and now offers to his father the precious relic that he is required to kiss."

Philip drew out the relic, and held it toward his father. As if a flash of lightning had passed through his mind, the captain of the vessel started back, clasped his hands, fell on his knees, and wept.

"My son, my son!" he exclaimed, rising and throwing himself into Philip's arms. "My eyes are opened—the Almighty knows how long they have been obscured."

Embracing each other, they walked aft, away from the men, who were still crowded at the gangway.

"My son, my noble son, before the charm is broken—before we resolve, as we must, into the elements—oh! let me kneel in thanksgiving and contrition. My son, my noble son, receive a father's thanks," exclaimed Vanderdecken. Then with tears of joy and penitence he humbly addressed himself to that Being Whom he once so awfully defied.

The elder Vanderdecken knelt down; Philip did the same; still embracing each other with one arm, they raised on high the other, and prayed.

For the last time the relic was taken from the bosom of Philip and handed to his father—and his father raised his eyes to heaven and kissed it. And as he kissed it, the long tapering upper spars of the Phantom vessel, the yards and sails that were set, fell into dust, fluttered in the air, and sank upon the wave. The mainmast, foremast, bowsprit, everything above the deck crumbled into atoms and disappeared.

Again Philip's father raised the relic to his lips, and the work of destruction continued. The heavy iron guns sank through the decks and disappeared; the crew of the vessel (who were looking on) crumbled down into skeletons, and dust, and fragments of ragged garments; and there were none left on board the vessel in the semblance of life but the father and son.

Once more did Philip's father put the sacred emblem to his lips. The beams and timbers separated, the decks of the vessel slowly sank, and the remnants of the hull floated upon the water. And as the father and son—the one young and vigorous, the other old and decrepit—still knelt, embracing, with their hands raised to heaven, and sank slowly under the deep blue wave, the lurid sky was for a moment illuminated by a lightning cross.

Then did the clouds which obscured the heavens roll away swift as thought—the sun again burst out in all its splendor—the rippling waves appeared to dance with joy. The screaming sea gull again whirled in the air, and the scared albatross once more slumbered on the wing. The porpoise tumbled and tossed in his sportive play, and albacore and dolphin leaped from the sparkling sea. All nature smiled as if it rejoiced that the charm was dissolved forever, and that THE PHANTOM SHIP WAS NO MORE.

The Yarn of the "Nancy Bell"

WILLIAM S. GILBERT

'Twas on the shores that round our coast
From Deal to Ramsgate span,
That I found alone on a piece of stone
An elderly naval man.

His hair was weedy, his beard was long,
And weedy and long was he,
And I heard this wight on the shore recite,
In a singular minor key;

"Oh, I am a cook, and the captain bold,
And the mate of the *Nancy* brig,
And a bo'sun tight, and a midshipmite,
And the crew of the captain's gig!"

And he shook his fists and he tore his hair,
Till I really felt afraid,
For I couldn't help thinking the man had been drinking,
And so I simply said;

"Oh, elderly man, it's little I know
Of the duties of men of the sea,
But I'll eat my hand if I understand
How you can possibly be

"At once a cook, and a captain bold,
And the mate of the *Nancy* brig,
And a bo'sun tight, and a midshipmite,
And the crew of the captain's gig."

Then he gave a hitch to his trousers, which
Is a trick all seamen larn,
And having got rid of a thumping quid,
He spun this painful yarn;

" 'Twas in the good ship *Nancy Bell*
That we sailed to the Indian sea,
And there on a reef we came to grief,
Which has often occurred to me.

"And pretty nigh all o' the crew was drowned
(There was seventy-seven o' soul),
And only ten of the *Nancy's* men
Said 'Here' to the muster roll.

"There was me and the cook and the captain bold,
And the mate of the *Nancy* brig,
And the bo'sun tight, and a midshipmite,
And the crew of the captain's gig.

"For a month we'd neither wittles nor drink,
Till a-hungry we did feel,
So we drawed a lot, and accordin' shot
The captain for our meal.

"The next lot fell to the *Nancy's* mate,
And a delicate dish he made;
Then our appetite with the midshipmite
We seven survivors stayed.

"And then we murdered the bo'sun tight,
And he much resembled pig;
Then we wittled free, did the cook and me,
On the crew of the captain's gig.

"Then only the cook and me was left,
And the delicate question 'which
Of us two goes to the kettle?' arose
And we argued it out as sich.

"For I loved that cook as a brother, I did,
And the cook he worshipped me;
But we'd both be blowed if we'd either be stowed
In the other chap's hold, you see.

" 'I'll be eat if you dines off me,' says Tom,
'Yes, that,' says I, 'you'll be!'
'I'm boiled if I die, my friend,' quoth I,
And 'Exactly so!' quoth he.

"Says he, 'Dear James, to murder me
Were a foolish thing to do,
For don't you see that you can't cook me,
While I can—and will—cook you?'

"So he boils the water and takes the salt
And the pepper in portions true
(Which he never forgot), and some chopped shalot,
And some sage and parsley, too.

" 'Come here,' says he, with proper pride,
Which his smiling features tell,
' 'Twill soothing be if I let you see,
How extremely nice you'll smell.'

164

"And he stirred it round and round and round
And he sniffed at the foaming froth;
When I ups with his heels, and smothers his squeals
In the scum of the boiling broth.

"And I eat that cook in a week or less,
And—as I eating be
The last of his chops, why, I almost drops,
For a vessel in sight I see.

"And I never grieve, and I never smile,
And I never larf nor play
But I sit and croak, and a single joke
I have—which is to say;

"Oh, I am a cook, and a captain bold,
And the mate of the *Nancy* brig,
And a bo'sun tight, and a midshipmite,
And the crew of the captain's gig!"

There was a bond between them and even death could not break it.

The Roll Call of the Reef

SIR ARTHUR QUILLER-COUCH

"Yes, sir," said my host the quarryman, reaching down the relics from their hook in the wall over the chimney piece, "they've hung there all my time, and most of my father's. The women won't touch 'em; they're afraid of the story. So here they'll dangle, and gather dust and smoke, till another tenant comes and tosses 'em out o' doors for rubbish. Whew! 'tis coarse weather."

He went to the door, opened it, and stood studying the gale that beat upon his cottage front straight from the Manacle Reef. The rain drove past him into the kitchen, aslant like threads of gold silk in the shine of the wreckwood fire. Meanwhile by the same firelight I examined the relics on my knee. The metal of each was tarnished out of knowledge. But the trumpet was evidently an old cavalry trumpet, and the threads of its parti-colored sling, though frayed and dusty, still hung together. Around the side drum, beneath its cracked brown varnish, I could hardly trace a royal coat-of-arms, and a legend running—*Per Mare per Terram*—the motto of the Marines. Its parchment, though colored and scented with wood smoke, was limp and mildewed; and I began to tighten up the straps—under which the drumsticks had been loosely thrust—with the idle purpose of trying if some music might be got out of the old drum yet.

But as I turned it on my knee, I found the drum attached to the trumpet sling by a curious barrel-shaped padlock, and paused to examine this. The body of the lock was composed of half a dozen brass rings, set accurately edge to edge; and, rubbing the brass with my thumb, I saw that each of the six had a series of letters engraved around it.

I knew the trick of it, I thought. Here was one of those word padlocks, once so common; only to be opened by getting the rings to spell a certain word, which the dealer confides to you.

My host shut and barred the door, and came back to the hearth.

" 'Twas just such a wind—east by south—that brought in what you've got between your hands. Back in the year 1809 it was; my father has told me the tale a score o' times. You're twisting the rings around, I see. But you'll never guess the word. Parson Kendall, he made the word, and locked down a couple o' ghosts in their graves with it; and when his time came, he went to his own grave and took the word with him."

"Whose ghosts, Matthew?"

"You want the story, I see, sir. My father could tell it better than I can. He was a young man in the year 'nine, unmarried at the time, and living in this very cottage just as I be. That's how he came to get mixed up with the tale."

He took a chair, lit a short pipe, and unfolded the story in a low musing voice, with his eyes fixed on the dancing violet flames.

"Yes, he'd ha' been about thirty year old in January of the year 'nine. The storm got up in the night o' the twenty-first o' that

170

month. My father was dressed and out long before daylight; he never was one to 'bide in bed, let be that the gale by this time was pretty near lifting the thatch over his head. Besides which, he'd fenced a small 'taty patch that winter, down by Lowland Point, and he wanted to see if it stood the night's work. He took the path across Gunner's Meadow—where they buried most of the bodies afterward. The wind was right in his teeth at the time, and once on the way (he's told me this often) a great strip of oar-weed came flying through the darkness and fetched him a slap on the cheek like a cold hand. But he made shift pretty well till he got to Lowland, and then had to drop upon his hands and knees and crawl, digging his fingers every now and then into the shingle to hold on, for he declared to me that the stones, some of them as big as a man's head, kept rolling and driving past till it seemed the whole foreshore was moving westward under him.

"The fence was gone, of course; not a stick left to show where it stood; so that, when first he came to the place, he thought he must have missed his bearings. My father, sir, was a very religious man; and if he reckoned the end of the world was at hand—there in the great wind and night, among the moving stones—you may believe he was certain of it when he heard a gun fired, and, with the same, saw a flame shoot up out of the darkness to windward, making a sudden fierce light in all the place about. All he could find to think or say was, 'The Second Coming—The Second Coming! The Bridegroom cometh, and the wicked He will toss like a ball into a large country!' And being already upon his knees, he just bowed his head and 'bided, saying this over and over.

"But by'm-by, between two squalls, he made bold to lift his head and look, and then by the light—a bluish color 'twas—he saw all the coast clear away to Manacle Point, and off the Manacles, in the thick of the weather, a sloop-of-war with topgallants housed, driving stern foremost towards the reef. It was she, of course, that was burning the flare. My father could see the white streak and the ports of her quite plain as she rose to it, a little outside the breakers,

171

and he guessed easy enough that her captain had just managed to wear ship, and was trying to force her nose to the sea with the help of her small bower anchor and the scrap or two of canvas that hadn't yet been blown out of her. But while he looked, she fell off, giving her broadside to it foot by foot, and drifting back on the breakers around Carn dû and the Varses. The rocks lie so thick thereabouts, that 'twas a tossup which she struck first. At any rate, my father couldn't tell at the time, for just then the flare died down and went out.

"Well, sir, he turned then in the dark and started back for Coverack to cry the dismal tidings—though well knowing ship and crew to be past any hope. And as he turned, the wind lifted him and tossed him forward 'like a ball,' as he'd been saying, and homeward along the foreshore. As you know, 'tis ugly work, even by daylight, picking your way among the stones there, and my father was prettily knocked about at first in the dark. But by then 'twas nearer seven than six o'clock, and the day spreading. By the time he reached North Corner, a man could see to read print. Hows'ever, he looked neither out to sea nor towards Coverack, but headed straight for the first cottage—the same that stands above North Corner today. A man named Billy Ede lived there then, and when my father burst into the kitchen bawling, 'Wreck! wreck!' he saw Billy Ede's wife, Ann, standing there in her clogs, with a shawl over her head, and her clothes wringing wet.

" 'Save the chap!' said Billy Ede's wife, Ann. 'What d' 'ee mean by crying stale fish at that rate?'

" 'But 'tis a wreck, I tell 'ee. I've a-zeed 'n!'

" 'Why, so 'tis,' said she, 'and I've a-zeed 'n too; and so has everyone with an eye in his head.'

"And with that she pointed straight over my father's shoulder, and he turned. And there, close under Dolor Point, at the end of Coverack town, he saw another wreck washing, and the point black with people, running to and fro in the morning light. While we stood staring at her, he heard a trumpet sounding on board, the notes coming in little jerks, like a bird rising against the wind; but faintly, of course, because of the distance and the gale blowing— though this had dropped a little.

" 'She's a transport,' said Billy Ede's wife, Ann, 'and full of horse soldiers, fine long men. When she struck they must ha' pitched the hosses over first to lighten the ship, for a score of dead hosses had washed in afore I left, half an hour back. An' three or four soldiers, too—fine long corpses in white breeches and jackets of blue and gold. I held the lantern to one. Such a straight young man.'

"My father asked her about the trumpeting.

" 'That's the queerest bit of all. She was burnin' a light when me an' my man joined the crowd down there. All her masts had gone; whether they were carried away, or were cut away to ease her, I don't rightly know. Anyway, there she lay 'pon the rocks with her decks bare. Her keelson was broke under her and her bottom sagged and stove, and she had just settled down like a sitting hen— just the leastest list to starboard; but a man could stand there easy. They had rigged up ropes across her, from bulwark to bulwark, an' beside these the men were mustered, holding on like grim death whenever the sea made a clean breach over them, an' standing up like heroes as soon as it passed. The captain an' the officers were clinging to the rail of the quarter-deck, all in their golden uniforms, waiting for the end as if 'twas King George they expected.

" 'There was no way to help, for she lay right beyond cast of line, though our folk tried it fifty times. And besides them clung a trumpeter, a whacking big man, an' between the heavy seas he would lift his trumpet with one hand, and blow a call; and every time he blew, the men gave a cheer. There (she says)—hark 'ee now—there he goes agen! But you won't hear no cheering any more, for few are left to cheer, and their voices weak. Bitter cold the wind is, and I reckon it numbs their grip o' the ropes, for they were dropping off fast with every sea when my man sent me home to get his breakfast. Another wreck, you say? Well, there's no hope for the tender dears, if 'tis the Manacles. You'd better run down and help yonder;

though 'tis little help that any man can give. Not one came in alive while I was there. The tide's flowing, an' she won't hold together another hour, they say.'

"Well, sure enough, the end was coming fast when my father got down to the point. Six men had been cast up alive, or just breathing—a seaman and five troopers. The seaman was the only one that had breath to speak; and while they were carrying him into the town, the word went round that the ship's name was the *Despatch,* transport, homeward bound from Corunna, with a detachment of the 7th Hussars that had been fighting out there with Sir John Moore. The seas had rolled her further over by this time, and given her decks a pretty sharp list; but a dozen men still held on, seven by the ropes near the ship's waist, a couple near the break of the poop, and three on the quarter-deck. Of these three my father made out one to be the skipper; close by him clung an officer in full regimentals—his name, they heard after, was Captain Duncanfield; the last came the tall trumpeter; and if you'll believe me, the fellow was making shift there, at the very last, to blow *'God save the King.'* What's more, he got to *'Send us victorious'* before an extra big sea came bursting across and washed them off the deck—every man but one of the pair beneath the poop—and *he* dropped his hold before the next wave; being stunned, I reckon. The others went out of sight at once, but the trumpeter—being, as I said, a powerful man as well as a tough swimmer—rose like a duck, rode out a couple of breakers, and came in on the crest of the third.

"The folks looked to see him broke like an egg at their feet; but when the smother cleared, there he was, lying face downward on a ledge below them; and one of the men that happened to have a rope round him—I forget the fellow's name, if I ever heard it—jumped down and grabbed him by the ankle as he began to slip back. Before the next big sea, the pair were hauled high enough to be out of harm, and another heave brought them up to grass. Quick work; but master trumpeter wasn't quite dead; nothing worse than

174

a cracked head and three staved ribs. In twenty minutes or so they had him in bed, with the doctor to tend him.

"Now was the time—nothing being left alive upon the transport—for my father to tell of the sloop he'd seen driving upon the Manacles. And when he got a hearing, though the most were set upon salvage, and believe a wreck in the hand, so to say, to be worth half a dozen they couldn't see, a good few volunteered to start off with him and have a look. They crossed Lowland Point; no ship to be seen on the Manacles, nor anywhere upon the sea. One or two was for calling my father a liar. 'Wait till we come to Dean Point,' said he. Sure enough, on the far side of Dean Point, they found the sloop's mainmast washing about with half a dozen men lashed to it—men in red jackets—every mother's son drowned and staring; and a little farther on, just under the Dean, three or four bodies cast up on the shore, one of them a small drummer boy, side drum and all; and, near by, part of a ship's gig, with 'H.M.S. *Primrose*' cut on the stern board. From this point on, the shore was littered with wreckage and dead bodies—most of them Marines in uniform; and in Godrevy Cove, in particular, a heap of furniture from the captain's cabin, and amongst it a watertight box, not much damaged, and full of papers, by which, when it came to be examined next day, the wreck was easily made out to be the *Primrose,* of eighteen guns, outward bound from Portsmouth, with a fleet of transports for the Spanish War—thirty sail, I've heard, but I've never heard what became of them. Being handled by merchant skippers, no doubt they rode out the gale and reached the Tagus safe and sound. Not but what the captain of the *Primrose* (Mein was his name) did quite right to try and club-haul his vessel when he found himself under the land: only he never ought to have got there if he took proper soundings. But it's easy talking.

"The *Primrose,* sir, was a handsome vessel—for her size, one of the handsomest in the King's service—and newly fitted out at

Plymouth Dock. So the boys had brave pickings from her in the way of brass work, ship's instruments, and the like, let alone some barrels of stores not much spoiled. They loaded themselves with as much as they could carry, and started for home, meaning to make a second journey before the preventive men got wind of their doings and came to spoil the fun. But as my father was passing back under the Dean, he happened to take a look over his shoulder at the bodies there. 'Hullo,' says he, and dropped his gear, 'I do believe there's a leg moving!' And, running fore, he stooped over the small drummer boy that I told you about. The poor little chap was lying there, with his face a mass of bruises and his eyes closed: but he had shifted one leg an inch or two, and was still breathing. So my father pulled out a knife and cut him free from his drum—that was lashed on to him with a double turn of Manilla rope—and took him up and carried him along here, to this very room that we're sitting in. He lost a good deal by this, for when he went back to fetch his bundle the preventive men had got hold of it, and were thick as thieves along the foreshore; so that 'twas only by paying one or two to look the other way that he picked up anything worth carrying off: which you'll allow to be hard, seeing that he was the first man to give news of the wreck.

"Well, the inquiry was held, of course, and my father gave evidence; and for the rest they had to trust to the sloop's papers, for not a soul was saved besides the drummer boy, and he was raving in a fever brought on by the cold and the fright. And the seamen and the five troopers gave evidence about the loss of the *Despatch*. The tall trumpeter, too, whose ribs were healing, came forward and kissed the Book; but somehow his head had been hurt in coming ashore, and he talked foolish-like, and 'twas easy seen he would never be a proper man again. The others were taken up to Plymouth, and so went their ways; but the trumpeter stayed on in Coverack; and King George, finding he was fit for nothing, sent him down a trifle of a pension after a while—enough to keep him in board and lodging, with a bit of tobacco over.

176

"Now the first time that this man—William Tallifer, he called himself—met with the drummer boy was about a fortnight after the little chap had bettered enough to be allowed a short walk out of doors, which he took, if you please, in full regimentals. There never was a soldier so proud of his dress. His own suit had shrunk a brave bit with the salt water; but into ordinary frock an' corduroys he declared he would not get—not if he had to go naked the rest of his life. So my father, being a good-natured man and handy with the needle, turned to and repaired damages with a piece or two of scarlet cloth cut from the jacket of one of the drowned Marines. Well, the poor little chap chanced to be standing, in this rig-out, down by the gate of Gunner's Meadow, where they had buried two score and over of his comrades. The morning was a fine one, early in March; and along came the cracked trumpeter, likewise taking a stroll.

"'Hullo!' says he; 'good mornin'! And what might you be doin' here?'

"'I was a-wishin',' says the boy, 'I had a pair o' drumsticks. Our lads were buried yonder without so much as a drum tapped or a musket fired; and that's not Christian burial for British soldiers.'

"'Phut!' says the trumpeter, and spat on the ground. 'A parcel of Marines!'

"The boy eyed him a second or so, and answered up: 'If I'd a tab of turf handy, I'd bung it at your mouth, you greasy cavalry-man, and learn you to speak respectful of your betters. The Marines are the handiest body of men in the service.'

"The trumpeter looked down on him from the height of six-foot-two, and asked: 'Did they die well?'

"'They died very well. There was a lot of running to and fro at first, and some of the men began to cry, and a few to strip off their clothes. But when the ship fell off for the last time, Captain Mein turned and said something to Major Griffiths, the commanding officer on board, and the Major called out to me to beat to quar-

177

ters. It might have been for a wedding, he sang it out so cheerful. We'd had word already that 'twas to be parade order, and the men fell in as trim and decent as if they were going to church. One or two even tried to shave at the last moment. The Major wore his medals. One of the seamen, seeing I had hard work to keep the drum steady—the sling being a bit loose for me and the wind what you remember—lashed it tight with a piece of rope; and that saved my life afterwards, a drum being as good as a cork until 'tis stove. I kept beating away until every man was on deck; and then the Major formed them up and told them to die like British soldiers, and the chaplain read a prayer or two—the boys standin' all the while like rocks, each man's courage keeping up the other's. The chaplain was in the middle of a prayer when she struck. In ten minutes she was gone. That was how they died, cavalryman.'

"'And that was very well done, drummer of the Marines. What's your name?'

"'John Christian.'

"'Mine is William George Tallifer, trumpeter, of the 7th Light Dragoons—the Queen's Own. I played *"God Save the King"* while our men were drowning. Captain Duncanfield told me to sound a call or two, to put them in heart; but that matter of *"God Save the King"* was a notion of my own. I won't say anything to hurt the feelings of a Marine, even if he's not much over five-foot tall; but the Queen's Own Hussars is a tearin' fine regiment. As between horse and foot, 'tis a question o' which gets the chance. So you played on your drum when the ship was goin' down? Drummer John Christian, I'll have to get you a new pair o' drumsticks for that.'

"Well, sir, it appears that the very next day the trumpeter marched into Helston, and got a carpenter there to turn him a pair of boxwood drumsticks for the boy. And this was the beginning of one of the most curious friendships you ever heard tell of. Nothing delighted the pair more than to borrow a boat off my father and pull out to the rocks where the *Primrose* and the *Des-*

178

patch had struck and sunk; and on still days 'twas pretty to hear them out there off the Manacles, the drummer playing his tattoo— for they always took their music with them—and the trumpeter practicing calls, and making his trumpet speak like an angel. But if the weather turned roughish, they'd be walking together and talking.

"But all this had to come to an end in the later summer; for the boy, John Christian, being now well and strong again, must go up to Plymouth to report himself. 'Twas his own wish (for I believe King George had forgotten all about him), but his friend wouldn't hold him back. As for the trumpeter, my father had made an arrangement to take him on as a lodger as soon as the boy left; and on the morning fixed for the start, he was up at the door here by five o'clock, with his trumpet slung by his side, and all the rest of his kit in a small valise. A Monday morning it was, and after breakfast he had fixed to walk with the boy some way on the road towards Helston, where the coach started. My father left them at breakfast together, and went out to do a few odd morning jobs. When he came back, the boy was still at table, and the trumpeter standing here by the chimney-place with the drum and trumpet in his hands, hitched together just as they be at this moment.

" 'Look at this,' he says to my father, showing him the lock; 'I picked it up off a starving brass worker in Lisbon, and it is not one of your common locks that one word of six letters will open at any time. There's *janius* in this lock; for you've only to make the rings spell any six-letter word you please, and snap down the lock upon that, and never a soul can open it—not the maker, even—until somebody comes along that knows the word you snapped it on. Now, Johnny here's goin', and he leaves his drum behind him; for, though he can make pretty music on it, the parchment sags in wet weather, by reason of the sea water getting at it; an' if he carries it to Plymouth, they'll only condemn it and give him another. And, as for me, I shan't have the heart to put lip to the

179

trumpet any more when Johnny's gone. So we've chosen a word together, and locked 'em together upon that; and, by your leave I'll hang 'em here together on the hook over your fireplace. Maybe Johnny'll come back; maybe not. Maybe, if he comes, I'll be dead an' gone, an' he'll take 'em apart an' try their music for old sake's sake. But if he never comes, nobody can separate 'em; for nobody beside knows the word. And if you marry and have sons, you can tell 'em that here are tied together the souls of Johnny Christian, drummer of the Marines, and William George Tallifer, once trumpeter of the Queen's Own Hussars. Amen.'

"With that he hung the two instruments 'pon the hook there; and the boy stood up and thanked my father and shook hands; and the pair went forth of the door, towards Helston.

"Somewhere on the road they took leave of one another; but nobody saw the parting, nor heard what was said between them. About three in the afternoon the trumpeter came walking back over the hill; and by the time my father came home from the fishing, the cottage was tidied up and the tea ready, and the whole place shining like a new pin. From that time for five years he lodged here with my father, looking after the house and tilling the garden; and all the while he was steadily failing, the hurt in his head spreading, in a manner, to his limbs. My father watched the feebleness growing on him, but said nothing. And from first to last neither spake a word about the drummer, John Christian; nor did any letter reach them, nor word of his doings.

"The rest of the tale you'm free to believe, sir, or not, as you please. It stands upon my father's words, and he always declared he was ready to kiss the Book upon it before judge and jury. He said, too, that he never had the wit to make up such a yarn; and he defied anyone to explain about the lock, in particular, by any other tale. But you shall judge for yourself.

"My father said that about three o'clock in the morning, April fourteenth of the year 1814, he and William Tallifer were sitting here, just as you and I, sir, are sitting now. My father had put on

180

his clothes a few minutes before. The trumpeter hadn't been to bed at all. Towards the last he mostly spent his nights (and his days, too) dozing in the elbow chair where you sit at this minute. He was dozing then (my father said), with his chin dropped forward on his chest, when a knock sounded upon the door, and the door opened, and in walked an upright young man in scarlet regimentals.

"He had grown a brave bit, and his face was the color of wood ashes; but it was the drummer, John Christian. Only his uniform was different from the one he used to wear, and the figures '38' shone in brass upon his collar.

"The drummer walked past my father as if he never saw him, and stood by the elbow chair and said:

"'Trumpeter, trumpeter, are you one with me?'

"And the trumpeter just lifted the lids of his eyes, and answered, 'How should I not be one with you, drummer Johnny—Johnny boy? The men are patient. 'Till you come, I count; while you march, I mark time; until the discharge comes.'

"'The discharge has come tonight,' said the drummer, 'and the word is Corunna no longer'; and stepping to the chimneyplace, he unhooked the drum and trumpet, and began to twist the brass rings of the lock, spelling the word aloud, so—C-O-R-U-N-A. When he had fixed the last letter, the padlock opened in his hand.

"'Did you know, trumpeter, that when I came to Plymouth they put me into a line regiment?'

"'The 38th is a good regiment,' answered the old Hussar, still in his dull voice. 'I went back with them from Sahagun to Corunna. At Corunna they stood in General Fraser's division, on the right. They behaved well.'

"'But I'd fain see the Marines again,' says the drummer, handing him the trumpet; 'and you—you shall call once more for the Queen's Own. Matthew,' he says, suddenly, turning on my father —and when he turned, my father saw for the first time that his scarlet jacket had a round hole by the breastbone, and that the

181

blood was welling there—'Matthew, we shall want your boat.'

"Then my father rose on his legs like a man in a dream, while they two slung on, the one his drum, and t'other his trumpet. He took the lantern, and went quaking before them down to the shore, and they breathed heavily behind him; and they stepped into his boat, and my father pushed off.

"'Row you first for Dolor Point,' says the drummer. So my father rowed them out past the white houses of Coverack to Dolor Point, and there, at a word, lay on his oars. And the trumpeter, William Tallifer, put his trumpet to his mouth and sounded the *Revelly*. The music of it was like rivers running.

"'They will follow,' said the drummer. 'Matthew, pull you now for the Manacles.'

"So my father pulled for the Manacles, and came to an easy close outside Carn dû. And the drummer took his sticks and beat a tattoo, there by the edge of the reef; and the music of it was like a rolling chariot.

"'That will do,' says he, breaking off; 'they will follow. Pull now for the shore under Gunner's Meadow.'

"Then my father pulled for the shore, and ran his boat in under Gunner's Meadow. And they stepped out, all three, and walked up to the meadow. By the gate the drummer halted and began his tattoo again, looking out towards the darkness over the sea.

"And while the drum beat, and my father held his breath, there came up out of the sea and the darkness a troop of many men, horse and foot, and formed up among the graves; and others rose out of the graves and formed up—drowned Marines with bleached faces, and pale Hussars riding their horses, all lean and shadowy. There was no clatter of hoofs or accoutrements, my father said, but a soft sound all the while, like the beating of a bird's wing, and a black shadow lying like a pool about the feet of all. The drummer stood upon a little knoll just inside the gate, and beside him the tall trumpeter, with hand on hip, watching them gather; and behind them both my father, clinging to the gate. When no more

182

came, the drummer stopped playing, and said, 'Call the roll.'

"Then the trumpeter stepped towards the end man of the rank and called, 'Troop-Sergeant-Major Thomas Irons!' and the man in a thin voice answered, 'Here!'

"'Troop-Sergeant-Major Thomas Irons, how is it with you?'

"The man answered, 'How should it be with me? When I was young, I betrayed a girl; and when I was grown, I betrayed a friend, and for these things I must pay. But I died as a man ought. God save the King!'

"The trumpeter called to the next man, 'Trooper Henry Buckingham!' and the next man answered, 'Here!'

"'Trooper Henry Buckingham, how is it with you?'

"'How should it be with me? I was a drunkard, and I stole, and in Lugo, in a wine shop, I knifed a man. But I died as a man should. God save the King!'

"So the trumpeter went down the line; and when he had finished, the drummer took it up, hailing the dead Marines in their order. Each man answered to his name, and each man ended with 'God save the King!' When all were hailed, the drummer stepped back to his mound, and called:

"'It is well. You are content, and we are content to join you. Wait yet a little while.'

"With this he turned and ordered my father to pick up the lantern, and lead the way back. As my father picked it up, he heard the ranks of dead men cheer and call, 'God save the King!' all together, and saw them waver and fade back into the dark, like a breath fading off a pane.

"But when they came back here to the kitchen, and my father set the lantern down, it seemed they'd both forgot about him. For the drummer turned in the lantern light—and my father could see the blood still welling out of the hole in his breast—and took the trumpet-sling from around the other's neck, and locked drum and trumpet together again, choosing the letters on the lock very carefully. While he did this he said:

183

"'The word is no more Corunna, but Bayonne. As you left out an "n" in Corunna, so must I leave out an "n" in Bayonne.' And before snapping the padlock, he spelt out the word slowly— 'B-A-Y-O-N-E.' After that, he used no more speech; but turned and hung the two instruments back on the hook; and then took the trumpeter by the arm; and the pair walked out into the darkness, glancing neither to right nor left.

"My father was on the point of following, when he heard a sort of sigh behind him; and there, sitting in the elbow chair, was the very trumpeter he had just seen walk out by the door! If my father's heart jumped before, you may believe it jumped quicker now. But after a bit, he went up to the man asleep in the chair, and put a hand upon him. It was the trumpeter in flesh and blood that he touched; but though the flesh was warm, the trumpeter was dead.

"Well, sir, they buried him three days after; and at first my father was minded to say nothing about his dream (as he thought it). But the day after the funeral, he met Parson Kendall coming from Helston market: and the parson called out: 'Have 'ee heard the news the coach brought down this mornin'?' 'What news?' says my father. 'Why, that peace is agreed upon.' 'None too soon,' says my father. 'Not soon enough for our poor lads at Bayonne,' the parson answered. 'Bayonne!' cries my father, with a jump. 'Why, yes'; and the parson told him all about a great sally the French had made on the night of April 13th. 'Do you happen to know if the 38th Regiment was engaged?' my father asked. 'Come, now,' said Parson Kendall, 'I didn't know you was so well up in the campaign. But, as it happens, I *do* know that the 38th was engaged, for 'twas they that held a cottage and stopped the French advance.'

"Still my father held his tongue; and when, a week later, he walked into Helston and bought a *Mercury* off the Sherborne rider, and got the landlord of the 'Angel' to spell out the list of killed and wounded, sure enough, there among the killed was Drummer John Christian, of the 38th Foot.

"After this, there was nothing for a religious man but to make a clean breast. So my father went up to Parson Kendall and told the whole story. The parson listened, and put a question or two, and then asked:

"'Have you tried to open the lock since that night?'

"'I han't dared to touch it,' says my father.

"'Then come along and try.' When the parson came to the cottage here, he took the things off the hook and tried the lock. 'Did he say *"Bayonne"*? The word has seven letters.'

"'Not if you spell it with one "n" as *he* did,' says my father.

"The parson spelt it out—B-A-Y-O-N-E. 'Whew!' says he, for the lock had fallen open in his hand.

"He stood considering it a moment, and then he says, 'I tell you what. I shouldn't blab this all round the parish, if I was you. You won't get no credit for truth telling, and a miracle's wasted on a set of fools. But if you like, I'll shut down the lock again upon a holy word that no one but me shall know, and neither drummer nor trumpeter, dead or alive, shall frighten the secret out of me.'

"'I wish to gracious you would, parson,' said my father.

"The parson chose the holy word there and then, and shut the lock back upon it, and hung the drum and trumpet back in their place. He is gone long since, taking the word with him. And till the lock is broken by force, nobody will ever separate those twain."

On Board the Derelict

YOUNG E. ALLISON

A Reminiscence of R. L. S.'s "Treasure Island"

Fifteen men on the dead man's chest—
    "Yo-ho-ho and a bottle of rum!
"Drink and the devil had done for the rest—
    "Yo-ho-ho and a bottle of rum!"
The mate was fixed by the bos'n's pike,
The bos'n brained with a marlinspike
And Cookey's throat was marked belike
    It had been gripped
        By fingers ten;
    And there they lay,
        All good dead men,
Like break-o'-day in a boozing-ken—
    Yo-ho-ho and a bottle of rum!

Fifteen men of a whole ship's list—
    Yo-ho-ho and a bottle of rum!
Dead and bedamned and the rest gone whist!—
    Yo-ho-ho and a bottle of rum!
The skipper lay with his nob in gore
Where the scullion's axe his cheek had shore—
And the scullion he was stabbed times four.
    And there they lay
        And the soggy skies
    Dripped all day long
        In up-staring eyes—

At murk sunset and at foul sunrise—
    Yo-ho-ho and a bottle of rum!

Fifteen men of 'em stiff and stark—
    Yo-ho-ho and a bottle of rum!
Ten of the crew had the Murder mark—
    Yo-ho-ho and a bottle of rum!
'Twas a cutlass swipe, or an ounce of lead,
Or a yawning hole in a battered head—
And the scuppers glut with a rotting red.
        And there they lay—
           Aye, damn my eyes!—
      All lookouts clapped
        On paradise—
All souls bound just contrariwise—
    Yo-ho-ho and a bottle of rum!

Fifteen men of 'em good and true—
    Yo-ho-ho and a bottle of rum!
Every man jack could ha' sailed with Old Pew—
    Yo-ho-ho and a bottle of rum!
There was chest on chest full of Spanish gold,
With a ton of plate in the middle hold,
And the cabins riot of stuff untold,
        And they lay there,
           That had took the plum,
        With sightless glare
           And their eyes struck dumb,
While we shared all by the rule of thumb—
    Yo-ho-ho and a bottle of rum!

More was seen through the sternlight screen—
    Yo-ho-ho and a bottle of rum!

Chartings no doubt where a woman had been!—
    Yo-ho-ho and a bottle of rum!
A flimsy shift on a bunker cot,
With a thin dirt slot through the bosom spot
And the lace stiff-dry in a purplish blot.
      Or was she a wench . . .
          Or some shuddering maid . . . ?
      That dared the knife—
          And that took the blade!
By God! she was stuff for a plucky jade—
    Yo-ho-ho and a bottle of rum!

"Fifteen men on the dead man's chest—
    "Yo-ho-ho and a bottle of rum!
"Drink and the devil had done for the rest—
    "Yo-ho-ho and a bottle of rum!"
We wrapped 'em all in a mains'l tight,
With twice ten turns of a hawser's bight,
And we heaved 'em over and out of sight—
      With a yo-heave-ho!
        And a fare-you-well!
      And a sullen plunge
        In the sullen swell
Ten fathoms deep on the road to hell!
    Yo-ho-ho and a bottle of rum!

They had hanged him and he was dead—but he had a long trip to make before he could lie in peace.

Anty Bligh

JOHN MASEFIELD

One night in the tropics I was "farmer" in the middle watch—that is, I had neither "wheel" nor "lookout" to stand during the four hours I stayed on deck. We were running down the Northeast Trades, and the ship was sailing herself, and the wind was gentle, and it was very still on board, the blocks whining as she rolled, and the waves talking, and the wheel chains clanking, and a light noise aloft of pattering and tapping. The sea was all pale with moonlight, and from the lamp-room door, where the watch was mustered, I could see a red stain on the water from the port side-light. The mate was walking the weather side of the poop, while the boatswain sat on the booby hatch humming an old tune and making a sheath for his knife. The watch were lying on the deck, out of the moonlight, in the shadow of the break of the poop. Most of them were sleeping, propped against the bulkhead. One of them was singing a new chanty he had made, beating out the tune with his pipe stem, in a little quiet voice that fitted the silence of the night.

> *Ha! Ha! Why don't you blow?*
> *O ho!*
> *Come, roll him over,*

repeated over and over again, as though he could never tire of the beauty of the words and the tune.

Presently he got up from where he was and came over to me. He was one of the best men we had aboard—a young Dane who talked English like a native. We had had business dealings during the dog watch, some hours before, and he had bought a towel from me, and I had let him have it cheap, as I had one or two to spare. He sat down beside me, and began a conversation, discussing a number of sailor matters, such as the danger of sleeping in the moonlight, the poison supposed to lurk in cold boiled potatoes, and the folly of having a good time in port. From these we passed to the consideration of piracy, coloring our talk with anecdotes of pirates.

"Ah, there was no pirate," said my friend, "like old Anty Bligh of Bristol. Dey hung old Anty Bligh off of the Brazils. He was the core and the strands of an old rogue, old Anty Bligh was. Dey hung old Anty Bligh on Fernando Noronha, where the prison is. And he walked after, Anty Bligh did. That shows how bad he was."

"How did he walk?" I asked. "Let's hear about him."

"Oh, they jest hung him," replied my friend, "like they'd hang any one else, and they left him on the gallows after. Dey thought old Anty was too bad to bury, I guess. And there was a young Spanish captain on the island in dem times. Frisco Baldo his name was. He was a terror. So the night dey hung old Anty, Frisco was

192

getting gorgeous wid some other captains in a kind of drinking shanty. And de other captains say to Frisco, 'I bet you a month's pay you won't go and put a rope round Anty's legs.' And 'I bet you a new suit of clothes you won't put a bowline around Anty's ankles.' And 'I bet you a cask of wine you won't put Anty's feet in a noose.' 'I bet you I will,' says Frisco Baldo. 'What's a dead man anyways,' he says, 'and why should I be feared of Anty Bligh? Give us a rope,' he says, 'and I'll lash him up wid seven turns, like a sailor would a hammock.'

"So he drinks up his glass, and gets a stretch of rope, and out he goes into the dark to where the gallows stood. It was a new moon dat time, and it was as dark as the end of a sea boot and as blind as the toe. And the gallows was right down by the sea dat time because old Anty Bligh was a pirate. So he comes up under the gallows, and there was old Anty Bligh hanging. And 'Way-ho, Anty,' he says. 'Lash and carry, Anty,' he says. 'I'm going to lash you up like a hammock.' So he slips a bowline around Anty's feet." . . . Here my informant broke off his yarn to light his pipe. After a few puffs he went on.

"Now when a man's hanged in hemp," he said gravely, "you mustn't never touch him with what killed him, for fear he should come to life on you. You mark that. Don't you forget it. So soon as ever Frisco Baldo sets that bowline around Anty's feet, old Anty looks down from his noose, and though it was dark, Frisco Baldo could see him plain enough. 'Thank you, young man,' said Anty; 'just cast that turn off again. Burn my limbs,' he says, 'if you ain't got a neck! And now climb up here,' he says, 'and take my neck out of the noose. I'm as dry as a cask of split peas.'

"Now you may guess that Frisco Baldo feller he come out all over in a cold sweat. 'Git a gait on you,' says Anty. 'I ain't going to wait up here to please you.' So Frisco Baldo climbs up, and a sore job he had of it getting the noose off Anty. 'Get a gait on you,' says Anty, 'and go easy with them clumsy hands of yours. You'll give me a sore throat,' he says, 'the way you're carrying on. Now don't let me fall plop,' says Anty. 'Lower away handsomely,' he says. 'I'll make you a weary one if you let me fall plop,' he says.

"So Frisco lowers away handsomely, and Anty comes to the ground, with the rope off him, only he still had his head to one side like he'd been hanged. 'Come here to me,' he says. So Frisco Baldo goes over to him. And Anty he jest put one arm round his neck, and gripped him tight and cold. 'Now march,' he says; 'march me down to the grog shop and get me a dram. None of your six-water dollops, neither,' he says; 'I'm as dry as a foul block,' he says. So Frisco and Anty they go to the grog shop, and all the while Anty's cold fingers was playing down Frisco's neck. And when they got to der grog shop der captains was all fell asleep. So Frisco takes the bottle of rum and Anty laps it down like he'd been used to it. 'Ah!' he says, 'thank ye,' he says, 'and now down to the Mole with ye,' he says, 'and we'll take a boat,' he says; 'I'm going to England,' he says, 'to say good-bye to me mother.'

"So Frisco he come out all over in a cold sweat, for he was feared of the sea; but Anty's cold fingers were fiddling on his neck, so he t'ink he better go. And when dey come to der Mole there was a boat there—one of these perry-acks, as they call them—and Anty he says, 'You take the oars,' he says. 'I'll steer,' he says, 'and every time you catch a crab,' he says, 'you'll get such a welt as you'll remember.' So Frisco shoves her off and rows out of the harbor, with old Anty Bligh at the tiller, telling him to put his beef on and to watch out he didn't catch no crabs. And he rowed, and he rowed, and he rowed, and every time he caught a crab—whack! he had it over the sconce with the tiller.

And der perry-ack it went a great holy big skyoot, ninety knots in der quarter of an hour, so they soon sees the Bull Point Light and der Shutter Light, and then the lights of Bristol. 'Oars,' said Anty. 'Lie on your oars,' he says; 'we got way enough.' Then dey make her fast to a dockside and dey goes ashore, and Anty has his arm round Frisco's neck, and 'March,' he says; 'step lively,' he says;

'for Johnny comes marching home,' he says. By and by they come to a little house with a light in the window. 'Knock at the door,' says Anty. So Frisco knocks, and in they go. There was a fire burning in the room and some candles on the table, and there, by the fire, was a very old, ugly woman in a red flannel dress, and she'd a ring in her nose and a black cutty pipe between her lips.

"'Good evening, Mother,' says Anty. 'I come home,' he says. But the old woman she just looks at him but never says nothing. 'It's your son Anty that's come home to you,' he says again.

"So she looks at him again and, 'Aren't you ashamed of yourself, Anty,' she says, 'coming home the way you are? Don't you repent your goings-on?' she says. 'Dying disgraced,' she says, 'in a foreign land, with none to lay you out.'

"'Mother,' he says, 'I repent in blood,' he says. 'You'll not deny me my rights?' he says.

"'Not since you repent,' she says. 'Them as repents I got no quarrel with. You was always a bad one, Anty,' she says, 'but I hoped you'd come home in the end. Well, and now you're come,' she says. 'And I must bathe that throat of yours,' she says. 'It looks as though you been hit by something.'

"'Be quick, Mother,' he says; 'it's after midnight now,' he says.

"So she washed him in wine, the way you wash a corpse, and put him in a white linen shroud, with a wooden cross on his chest, and two silver pieces on his eyes, and a golden marigold between his lips. And together they carried him to the perry-ack and laid him in the stern sheets.

"'Give way, young man,' she says; 'give way like glory. Pull, my heart of blood,' she says, 'or we'll have the dawn on us.'

"So he pulls, that Frisco Baldo does, and the perry-ack makes big southing—a degree a minute—and they comes ashore at the Mole just as the hens was settling to their second sleep.

"'To the churchyard,' says the old woman; 'you take his legs.' So they carries him to the churchyard at the double.

"'Get a gait on you,' says Anty. 'I feel the dawn in my bones,'

195

he says. 'My wraith'll chase you if you ain't in time,' he says.

"And there was an empty grave, and they put him in, and shoveled the clay, and the old woman poured out a bottle on the top of it. 'It's holy water,' she says. 'It's to make his wraith rest easy.' Then she runs down to the sea's edge and gets into the perry-ack. And immediately she was hull down beyond the horizon, and the sun came up out of the sea, and the cocks cried cock-a-doodle in the hen roost, and Frisco Baldo falls down into a swound. He was a changed man from that out."

"Lee for brace," said the mate above us. "Quit your chinning there, and go forward to the rope."

Full Fathom Five

Full fathom five thy father lies;
    Of his bones are coral made;
Those are pearls that were his eyes:
    Nothing of him that doth fade
But doth suffer a sea-change
Into something rich and strange.
Sea-nymphs hourly ring his knell.
        Ding-dong. Ding dong bell.

Ariel's Song from *The Tempest*
by William Shakespeare

About the Stories
and Authors

ROBERT ARTHUR was born on the faraway island of Corregidor, in the Philippines. He graduated from the University of Michigan to become a writer of short stories, radio and television programs, and juvenile books. In *Jabez O'Brien and Davy Jones' Locker* he has given us a sprightly view of the fabled Davy Jones and his Locker, as seen through the eyes of a New England fisherman. Despite the fact that Davy Jones is a legendary sea character known to almost everyone, this is one of the rare stories in which he appears.

LORD DUNSANY, born in 1878, served in the Boer War and World War I. Before his death in 1957, he wrote many short stories, plays and novels, most of them tales of fantasy based on a mythology of his own creation. He was particularly deft in writing brief, imaginative short stories. *One August in the Red Sea* is one of a number he wrote using the character Joseph Jorkens as a narrator.

WILLIAM OUTERSON was born in Edinburgh and ran off to sea when in his teens. During the Spanish-American War he saw action in the U.S. Navy. Later he prospected for gold in Alaska, practiced law in Scotland, and soldiered in World War I. From 1922 until his death in 1943 he wrote short stories. *Fire in the Galley Stove* was suggested to him by the famous mystery of the *Mary Celeste,* a sailing ship found abandoned in 1872, under sail and with full stores of food and water aboard. There was even laundry still hanging from a line. In his story Capt. Outerson has imagined a surprise attack by a vast marine monster that sweeps captain and crew from a ship without leaving a trace.

201

Probably no one has ever seen a miniature ship under full sail inside a bottle without wondering, with admiration, how it came there. Even knowing the answer—that the ships are built inside the bottle with long tweezers, one tiny piece at a time—does not detract from the curious spell such ships exert. In *Ship-In-A-Bottle,* P. SCHUYLER MILLER has translated the mystery of these ships into a story of real magic, a real ship enchanted into a bottle. Mr. Miller, born in Troy, N.Y., and trained as a chemist, has done most of his work in the field of public relations, educational radio and advertising and technical writing. Along the way he has written stories of science fiction and fantasy, of which this is one of his finest.

The legend of the Flying Dutchman, the ship that sails endlessly and can never reach port, is a very old one. In *The Flying Dutchman,* AUGUSTE JAL has related how the legendary vessel acquired its curse. Mr. Jal, a French writer of the last century, wrote a great deal about the sea, and undoubtedly took older legends and tales and made them the basis for this story.

FRANK BELKNAP LONG is a contemporary editor and writer who has done much work in the field of science fiction and the fantastic. He has been recently represented by such collections of his work as *The Dark Beasts* and *The Hounds of Tindalos. Second Night Out,* with its finely sustained atmosphere of enigmatic horror, is widely regarded as one of his best works.

STEPHEN VINCENT BENET (1898–1943) was dedicated to literature from his college days. He had published two books of poems before he was 18. His best known poem, *John Brown's Body,* appeared in 1928 and won a Pulitzer prize. His short story *The Devil and Daniel Webster* is an acknowledged minor classic. His mastery of vivid English is well shown in his piratical poem, *The Hemp,* which has been deleted somewhat, by permission, for publication here.

WILLIAM HOPE HODGSON specialized in supernatural stories and dramatic, colorful stories of the sea. His death in World War I, in 1918, cut short a promising career that might have brought us many more stories touched with his own distinctive style and imagination. *The Stone Ship* and *The Voice in the Night* represent his special approach to the sea as a place of wonder and mystery where nothing is impossible.

ALFRED NOYES, born in England in 1880, for more than 50 years wrote novels, essays, plays, short stories and children's novels. He is best known today for his poetry, his *The Highwayman* being a great favorite. Since *Forty Singing Seamen* was first published in this country in 1906, it has been a favorite with readers of all ages for the lilt of its lines and the colorful adventure it tells of. Mr. Noyes died in 1958.

CAPTAIN FREDERICK MARRYAT (1792–1848) wrote many tales of high nautical adventure which were soundly based on personal experience. He entered the English navy at 14, and in two and a half years as a midshipman took part in more than 50 naval engagements. When he started to write, his experience gave his work great authenticity. *The Phantom Ship* is undoubtedly based upon the same legends as *The Flying Dutchman*, by Auguste Jal, who was writing at about the same time. In contrast, however, it is a full length novel, of which only a brief portion is printed here.

WILLIAM S. GILBERT (1836–1911), who wrote *The Yarn of the Nancy Bell* as one of his famous *Bab Ballads,* is better known as the man who, in partnership with Sir Arthur Sullivan, wrote the comic operas *The Mikado, H.M.S. Pinafore,* and many others. Almost all of his work was in a humorous vein, and he had great dexterity in presenting amusingly topsy-turvy ideas in deft and catchy rhymes.

SIR ARTHUR QUILLER-COUCH (1863–1944) spent his whole life as a writer and a teacher of literature. He was commissioned to complete the novel *St. Ives,* which Robert Louis Stevenson began and died without finishing. Much of his work is seldom read today, but *The Roll Call of the Reef* remains a vivid token of his ability to write with drama and imagination.

YOUNG E. ALLISON was a Kentucky man who all his life enjoyed tales of treasure and piracy. When *Treasure Island* was first published, Mr. Allison was especially intrigued by the four lines of verse that appear throughout the book, beginning, "Fifteen men on a dead man's chest. . . ." In the book these lines are referred to as the verse of a much longer ballad. Mr. Allison set himself to write the ballad that author Robert Louis Stevenson only hinted at. The result was the publication in 1891 of a song, *A Piratical Ballad,* with words by Young E. Allison and music by a friend. Mr. Allison continued to work on the ballad, and expanded it into a poem, *On Board The Derelict,* which appeared in *The Rubric* (Chicago) in 1901. In the years immediately after it was published it was widely reprinted, often without credit to the author. It is said that the author wrote two additional verses but was not satisfied with them and never released them for publication.

JOHN MASEFIELD, born in England in the same year as Lord Dunsany, 1878, went to sea in an English training ship when he was 13. In his teens he sailed around Cape Horn on a freighter. After following the sea for several years, he turned to literature, writing many stories and poems that concerned the sea. In 1930 he was appointed poet laureate of England by King George V. *Anty Bligh* is one of a group of his earlier stories, told vividly and with great economy of words.

Other Popular Random House Anthologies of
Mystery and Suspense Stories for Young Readers